Clea's father took know that Delos belo choosing his words ca than you could imagine. Delos couldn't have learned it, because it comes from within."

The room was silent.

"Look at the star on your right palm, Clea. Delos has one, too. He is Skyborn." Taland met her gaze. "And so are you."

OMNI

SKYBORN

MARCIA H. KRUCHTEN

SCHOLASTIC INC.
New York Toronto London Auckland Sydney

In loving memory of my father,
Donald Earl Chambers,
who always had a book in his hand.

ISBN 0-590-40279-X

12 11 10 9 8 7 6 5 4 3 2 1   9/8 0 1 2 3 4/9

Printed in the U.S.A.   01

First Scholastic printing, February 1989

Chapter 1

"Clea . . . *Cle-e-e-a!*"

The voice echoed past the girl sitting in the shadow of the thick white wall of the palace. She ignored it and dug her toes through the grass, into the warm loamy soil. Resting her chin on her knees, she looked down past the gleaming walls of the three harbors that circled the rise on which the palace stood.

Clea could see two bulky gray beasts below. From where she sat, the animals looked no larger than the palm of her hand. Their long, fingerlike noses swayed before them as they moved toward a wide barge stacked with wood. Fascinated, she watched them wrap their noses about the beams, lifting them up one by one. Incredible.

Clea's eyes glowed as she took in each detail. When the slaves had told her of the animals, she had scoffed. She knew they couldn't exist, not in Atlantis, for she had never heard of them. At last an old water-tender had told her with asperity where they might be seen, and she had gone to look for herself at once.

"No eyes to see with if she will not use them,"

the old man had muttered — under his breath, of course. She smiled faintly, and then wondered again why even the servants knew more than she did. It wasn't a new question, but one that troubled her more often lately.

Clea watched the great harbor below, hoping to see something else new, but there was nothing. She played absently with her new gold necklace as she thought about her situation. The few students with whom she took classes came up the hill to the temple in the morning and then went wherever they pleased for the rest of the day. But not Clea. The merchants' market beyond the busy harbor might as well have been a fantasy. All she knew of it were stories gleaned from the palace slaves.

A hand came down on Clea's shoulder, and she jumped. Nera stood huffing over her. Her dark hair clung in wet circles to her neck, and her cheeks were brilliant from hurrying.

"Clea, you . . ." Nera panted, fanning herself with her plump hands, "You should be punished." She completely lost her breath, and Clea laughed.

"Couldn't you find me, Nera?" she teased. "Did you think I'd run away to find a ship of my own?" She nodded at the harbor. "I was watching the long-noses unload wood."

"Biros sent me to find you," Nera said. "I don't see any long-noses. Come on, Clea." Her voice was flat.

Clea looked up, surprised. "Oh, Nera, look there," she said impatiently. She pointed to the left of the small temple below them on the slope. "There, past the second sentry post. Two of them, see?"

Nera looked uneasily toward the harbor and then at the sky, fiercely clear and blue. "There's nothing there. And it's past time for our lessons, they've already begun."

Clea's eyes narrowed. Why would Nera deny that the animals were there? It was impossible to miss them. Nera was still talking, babbling about nothing, as she hauled Clea to her feet.

Clea twisted away, annoyed. "You forget yourself," she said coldly.

"Oh, be still," Nera snapped. "Just look at your drape. See how dusty you've gotten it?" She began to pull Clea toward the front of the palace with offended little jerks. "I wonder why you even bother to go to class," she went on crossly. "You don't seem to appreciate it. It's a waste. Rhanjhon — "

"Oh, Rhanjhon. I'm sick of hearing the name. How do you know he even exists?" Clea pushed Nera's hand from her arm as her companion grew pale at this blasphemy. "Wait," Clea commanded. There was a familiar tremor in the air, something more easily felt than heard. A message. From her father. *Yes, Father. I am coming,* Clea sent back.

"My father wants to see me," Clea said, turning away. "The priest can wait." And with that she ran up the wide stone steps and into the palace, leaving Nera staring after her. Nera would have to make excuses to their teacher, the priest Biros.

"It serves her right, too," Clea murmured. "She has no right to talk to me like that." Although Biros would scold Nera for returning without her, he wouldn't strike her. As Clea's companion, Nera was protected. She grinned, thinking of Biros's temper.

There are some advantages to being the King's granddaughter, she thought grimly, even if I can't leave the Citadel.

The palace halls were cool and dim away from the glare of the sun. Clea pattered along them, taking the turns to her father's study automatically. She stopped beneath a newly completed fresco, glancing up at it. It showed row on row of men and women carrying tribute to a badly painted King. Clea wished the artist had made her grandfather look more like himself.

She remembered watching the artist with envy, longing to paint the wall herself. She knew her sketches were the best in her class, but the painter had still denied her request. Waving at the outline of the King on the wall, he had said, "No, not you."

Her throat tightened. It seemed she never got to do anything she really wanted to do. She would complain to her father again, though it wouldn't do any good. He would simply look at her with a puzzled frown, then go back to his scrolls and forget all about it until the next time.

Clea turned toward her father's workroom and pulled open the heavy door. She burst into the familiar roofless room and stopped abruptly.

Taland sat at the slender table he had designed himself, facing a fresh sheet of rolled clay. He put aside the tool with which he worked and stood up.

Clea flushed, knowing her father could tell she was angry. Well, why not? she argued with herself. What good did it do to pretend?

"Why can't *I* do a fresco?" Clea flared. "I could have done as well as the last painter we had. You know my designs are good. It's just not fair. And besides," she rushed on, "Nera said there weren't any long-noses down by the harbor, and that's stupid. There were, I saw them."

"Elephants," Taland put in mildly.

"Well, elephants, then. Why don't I learn about elephants in my classes? I'm tired of Biros, and I'm tired of never going anywhere. All Biros does is talk on and on about Rhanjhon and the blessing of Atlantis, and I'm not even sure. . . ." She stopped guiltily, afraid to continue.

Her father sighed. "Clea," he said, "please sit. Apparently there is more going on than the poor lessons Biros complains about. I think we need to talk."

As Taland closed the door, Clea crossed the small bare room and threw herself on a pillowed bench, mutinous. Taland pulled his stool over and sat down.

"You've never had any patience," Clea's father told her. "Even as a babe. I remember so well. Perhaps your mother was right. Perhaps one can't mold a pot from a sword. . . ."

Clea rolled over and put her chin on her hands. It was rare for Taland to speak of her mother, and Clea had learned early not to ask questions. Too often she had been answered with silence, or a sigh. She could barely remember her mother, and then only as a presence, not as an actual memory. While she was grateful to have her father and grandfather, that didn't change the fact that she was completely bored.

"Is it because Grandfather is King that I can't do anything?" Clea asked. She was questioning herself more than her father, for it was the sort of question he never seemed to hear.

Yet Taland answered, which surprised her. "Clea, there are things you don't know," he said gravely. "I thought you were too young to be told, that's all. There are matters that concern the way you've been raised. I didn't realize you were so unhappy." Clea flushed, wondering what on earth he was talking about.

"Your grandfather and I thought Nera would keep you from being so lonely," Taland went on. "And as for Nera's ignoring your elephants, well . . . she's been told not to encourage your curiosity. You know it isn't safe for you to go about alone. We felt perhaps the less you knew about the world, the more safe you would be." He shook his head. "You're growing up," he said, rising.

Clea jumped to her feet. "But you haven't told me anything!" she cried. "If there are things I should know, why not just tell me?" Taland had always been vague, but never so mysterious.

Taland hugged Clea instead of answering her question, and he smoothed her straight dark hair. Clea couldn't remember the last time he had done that. "I'll have to talk with your grandfather first," he said. "Right now I want you to go to class. Don't frown, Clea. It won't hurt you to be pleasant to Biros. But remember this. Don't speak to anyone about what we've said here. Not even Nera. It's important." His face was remote, and Clea knew the conversation was over — at least, for now.

Chapter 2

I suppose I'd better go to class, Clea thought gloomily. Forcing her attention back to her duty, she slipped out of the palace into the mid-morning heat. Her laggard steps turned east toward the temple.

After reaching it, Clea stopped in the high arched opening. She hated to enter. Instead, she looked longingly down toward the swarming harbor.

Everything that could possibly be thought of must be there. Ships came and went, people quarreled and laughed and did whatever they pleased, merchants sold goods from all over the world — or so Nera had carelessly said once. When Clea kept after her, Nera wouldn't speak of it again, remarking spitefully that some people didn't know when they were well off; some people should show gratitude for their blessings; some people. . . . So Clea gave up, knowing it wasn't likely she'd learn more. Not from Nera.

Clea remembered something from childhood. Someone had once given her a fluttering bird when she was ill and restless with fever. It had beaten its bright wings against the bars of its cage until, in a spasm of pity, she had run across the room to free it. The thought was uncomfortable.

Biros's harsh voice rose from the temple. Clea grimaced. He might be the High Priest of Rhanjhon, but he was also quite dull. Why couldn't he let one of the more interesting priests teach?

When the voice paused, the class chanted the responses. Clea whispered the words with them. "Rhanjhon our god did cause the world to tremble and the towers of the mighty to topple." Biros spoke again, and again she whispered with the other voices. "The wrath of our god was great and terrible, but for his island he put out his hand in peace, and Atlantis he blessed. . . ."

Suddenly, without warning, a small furry form hurtled into Clea's legs, tangling her clothing. She fell helplessly through the opening. The creature danced, shrieked, flung its arms at her in apparent rage, and flew into the gloom of the hallway.

She stared after the animal, astonished. How ugly its face was! It looked like a withered old man, but had bright beady eyes. She'd never seen anything like it.

Sandals pounded on the path. A boy with a dirty cloth about his waist slid to a stop by Clea's knee.

"Where is he?" the boy demanded. "Did you see which way he went?" Clea jumped to her feet, but before she could answer, she heard screams and shouting in the temple. The boy darted into the temple toward the uproar, and Clea limped after him, excited. Biros would be angry at the intrusion, and that could be entertaining.

She caught up with the boy at the first turn in the hall, where he stood, confused. It was clear that he wasn't familiar with the temple. Clea touched his arm before she saw it was mottled with dirt and who knew what else. She snatched her hand back in distaste. The babble from the classroom was loud.

"There," Clea said, pointing to the door the boy wanted, the only one of the four doors behind the altar room marked with a trident. The boy rushed across the floor and jerked the handle.

As the door slowly swung open, Biros appeared, half-crouching, ten paces away. His dark face was a peculiar yellowish-gray. The wild-eyed creature holding on to his oiled hair screeched at the students attempting to beat it away. Clea began to laugh.

"No!" shouted the boy. "Boca, come here." The animal flung itself over the heads of the students, landing in his arms. The boy smoothed its fur as it nestled against his bare brown shoulder.

Biros strode toward them ponderously, his azure robe swirling. He pushed the boy aside roughly. "I'll send for a guard," the priest snarled. "If you leave, boy, it will be the worse for you. I promise."

"And if I stay, all will be well?" The boy's clear voice held contempt, but no fear. Biros spun back to him, his arm raised to strike.

"You shall not do this." Clea was surprised to find herself standing between Biros and the stranger, her chin lifted in defiance.

Biros's heavy neck swelled and reddened. The look he gave Clea might have terrified her if she hadn't been so sure of her immunity. "You go too far," Biros said softly. "Out of my way."

"Clea . . ." Nera gasped, clutching at her arm.

Oddly calm, Clea shook Nera's hand away. "The boy means no harm," she said. "The creature is his. Do you really need a guard to prove it, Biros?"

"The creature is dangerous," Biros hissed. "I need a guard to wring its neck, to guarantee the safety of my students. As for this" — he paused, glancing at the boy with a sneer — "this . . . harbor rat, isn't it? Since you so ardently desire his safety, I will allow him to return unharmed to his own filth."

The boy flushed slightly, but otherwise showed no sign of having heard a word Biros said. Clea was impressed, since she knew she would be seething in his place, and worse, wouldn't be able to hide it.

"You frightened the creature, Biros," Clea said sweetly. "See? It's content in its master's arms. You can see it's hardly dangerous. Oh, by the way, I almost forgot. I have a message for you from my father. He asks that I be excused from class. He needs me." The words seemed to say themselves. She certainly hadn't planned to lie. Her heart pounded so loudly she was sure Biros could hear it.

Biros's hooded gaze was skeptical. "You're sure?" he questioned. "He said nothing to me, Clea."

"Do you doubt my word?" Clea countered, not knowing what else to say. She plunged on, ignoring Nera's horrified look. "I will take the creature and its master to the palace. My father wishes to see them. Please continue without me." With that, she left the room. The boy followed.

Clea heard the stone door thud shut behind them. She let out her breath and glanced at her companion. The boy smiled broadly. Clea realized with a start that his eyes looked just like hers.

"Who are you then?" Clea whispered.

"I'm no one you would know. I'm a harbor rat,

remember?" he replied, his smile gone. He walked steadily through the arch and out into the sun. Clea had to skip to keep up with him.

"But why are you here? And what is this creature of yours?" Clea persisted.

"You don't know this is an old one?" he asked, surprised. She shook her head, putting out her hand to touch the animal. It turned its wise little face to hers and made a low chirring sound.

"I call him Boca," the boy said. "He ran away, bad creature, and I chased him here." He shook his pet in annoyance and smiled when it scolded him for it. "Surely you know about these animals?" Clea shook her head again. "A seaman I know gave him to me for helping unload his ship. He comes from far away. He was just a rack of bones after the long voyage, but I fed him from my own hand. You did well, eh, Boca?" He rubbed his cheek across the old one's ear. "He came from the land of high pyramids." When he saw she didn't know what he was talking about, he looked away.

"I simply hadn't seen one before," Clea said quickly. "So it has a name and you don't?" she went on, changing the subject. "How odd."

"I didn't say that," the boy said coolly. "They call me Delos."

"Where do you live? What does your father do?" Clea asked, consumed by curiosity.

The boy stared at her. "I didn't come up here to entertain you. I came after Boca. I've already said that. And I don't want to speak with your father, either. We both know he doesn't even know me."

Clea's cheeks reddened. While she still couldn't

believe she'd lied about that to Biros, she hadn't expected to be judged by a nobody for it. It was enough to imagine what her father would say.

"I don't mean to be ungrateful," Delos went on. "The lie saved Boca's neck. But since I've no business here, I'll be leaving." He strode away down the path toward the first bridge.

Clea ran after him. "Wait," she cried. She wasn't sure why, but she knew he couldn't leave. Perhaps it was because he was from the harbor. He would know so many things — things Nera refused to tell her. "My father would like to meet you, Delos, truly," she insisted. "Can't we just show him the old one? It will amuse him." She pulled at his arm impatiently. "Please?"

Delos studied her and shrugged. "Why not?" he asked. "I have nothing better to do this morning."

Boca peered over the boy's shoulder as they went up the steps into the palace. The creature's soft chattering made an eerie sound in the echoing silence.

Clea ran lightly through the halls, but Delos lagged behind. He bent to touch the pale lilies and languid reeds in the mosaic floor and stared at the walls as if he had never seen a painted swallow before. So, there are things *he* hasn't seen, Clea thought, obscurely pleased. Delos saw her watching him and quickened his step. He was just behind her when she flung open the door to Taland's workroom, a hasty greeting on her lips.

But the sound choked in Clea's throat. A great golden light poured from the open door, striking her face. She fell back with a cry. Delos leapt to catch her, as Boca ran away, shrieking in fear.

A figure stood within the room, surrounded by a bright, pulsing glow. It seemed to be a man, but the form was misty and unclear, transparent. Clea could see the stone of the wall through him.

Chapter 3

Delos cried out in a foreign language as Clea threw her hands across her eyes, twisting her head aside. Flinging her hands away, she stared into the room. "Father," she screamed, the sound muffled and strange to her ears.

At the sound of her voice, the brilliant yellow haze surrounding the figure shattered. Tiny flickering fires spun away, to be lost in the air. The small room was bathed in ordinary sunlight again. At the breaking of the glow, Taland fell heavily to the floor, but not before Clea saw him look toward the door. Pain and joy were written on his face.

With a strangled sob, Clea ran to her father. He was unconscious, but his eyes were open and his gaze fixed. She moved her hand before his eyes, but they didn't blink. She was too frightened to speak.

Delos knelt to feel Taland's chest. He bent forward. "He's breathing. His heart's beating well."

"Quickly, Delos, get some water," Clea ordered. "And a cloth. Bring a cloth." She watched her father anxiously.

Delos rose, but made no move to obey her. When she looked up, impatient, she saw he was angry. "I'll help you with your father," he said. "But I'm not a slave, and I don't like the way you speak to me."

Clea's face was red. "If you're quite done," she retorted, "then help me instead of just standing there. Can't you see my father may be dying?"

Delos shrugged. "I don't think he's in any danger if he's still breathing," he said. "Your name is Clea? You didn't bother to tell me, but the High Priest called you that. Well, Clea, I think I'd better close the door first. I've heard these priests don't care for those who weave spells with the dead."

"You're mad," Clea gasped. "There's no evil in this room."

"What do you call what we saw?" Delos asked. He moved silently to the hall and returned with Boca, barring the door securely behind him. "Where's the water?" he asked.

Clea jerked her head toward a small room, which opened onto the workroom, answering his last question with this gesture. The first question couldn't be answered, for the golden mist they had seen couldn't be explained. There was no point in thinking about it until Taland woke up. *If* he wakes up, she thought, shuddering.

As she scrambled to her feet, her sandal caught a round object lying by her father, sending it skittering into a corner. She ran to pick it up. It was heavy — a flat engraved disc of some red metal she hadn't seen before. She dropped it on Taland's table and flew through the door to find Delos looking at the shelves, instead of getting water.

Clea was furious. "Is this the way you help?" she snapped, giving the boy a shove as she snatched up an empty pitcher. She plunged it into the water basin and reached for a folded cloth from the stack on the stained counter. As she ran back, water trailed behind her, splashing with each step.

After Clea bathed Taland's face and wrists, he groaned, and his eyes closed.

"Could we move him?" Delos asked. "He'd be more comfortable on that bench." He worked an arm under Taland's shoulders and between them, they managed to carry him across the room. Delos wedged a pillow beneath Taland's head while Boca leaped to the foot of the bench.

Delos turned to Clea. "Has your father ever been ill like this before? I mean, has anything like this ever happened?"

She shook her head. "Never. I don't know what to think, Delos. That glow. . . . Well, it was like something was wrong with the sun." Clea glanced up as if expecting to see a ring of sunlight descending, but there was nothing frightening above her. The sky was as it always was, intensely blue with wisps of cloud.

Then she looked back at her father and caught her breath. He was awake and watching Delos.

"Your hand. . . ." Taland said huskily. "Hand." Startled, Delos stepped back lightly. "Leo?" Taland went on, his clouded gaze intent on the boy.

"Father," Clea said sharply. "Father, this is Clea. I'm here, Father." Had his mind fled along with the tiny sun fires? His words meant nothing. She reached to touch him, but he moved away.

Delos, wary, picked up Boca in the crook of his arm. Taland watched the creature for a long moment, his face puzzled. When he looked back at Delos, his eyes were clear.

What is your name? Clea felt her father say. Delos made no response. But of course he wouldn't, Clea thought, confused. Taland had always told her this was their secret speech. Why would he expect this harbor boy to be able to use it? It was obvious Delos hadn't heard, or he would have responded.

Taland spoke. "Your name?" His voice, though weak, was his own, and demanded an answer.

"It's Delos," the boy replied.

"Your home?" Taland sat up, rubbing his forehead as if it ached.

"I have no home. I stay with friends," Delos said, glancing at Clea.

Taland hesitated. Then, "Your parents?" he asked, his manner somehow different.

"I have none. I work, I feed myself. I'm my own master," Delos replied, his face darkening. "Who are you to wonder at it?"

Clea caught her breath. Why would her father question this boy? Why didn't he take offense at Delos's manner? It wasn't like Taland. And he'd hardly looked at Clea. She felt a barb of jealousy. "Father," she cried.

Taland silenced her, swinging his legs over the edge of the bench. He stood unsteadily, still watching Delos. "Give me your hand," he said.

Delos looked away in annoyance. At last he thrust out his hand. Instead of holding it, Taland turned it over to look at the palm. "Ah."

What purpose could this have? Clea didn't see anything remarkable about the boy's hand but that his nails were dirty and broken. Why was Taland ignoring her, his own daughter? Clea sat down suddenly on a stool, morose.

"Clea, don't fret," Taland told her. "You don't understand what has happened here. I will remedy your ignorance, I promise you."

Ignorance? Why, she was better at memorizing than anyone in Biros's classes. Clea opened her mouth to argue, but before she could speak, a harsh voice demanded admittance. It was Biros, of course. Sometimes he acted as if Clea were put on earth specifically for his guidance.

Taland rolled his eyes skyward and moved to unbar the door. "Yes, Biros," he said, abrupt but courteous. "I am occupied. Do you have a message for me?"

Biros, taller and heavier than Clea's father, peered past his shoulder into the room. His nostrils flared with dislike as he saw Delos standing with Clea.

"I see your daughter is here," Biros said. "She told me you needed her." Clea held her breath, but the priest rushed on, not giving her father time to reply. "Let me remind you that I have spoken to you about Clea's disruptive attitude." His voice flattened like an ooze of oil. "We do have rules. One royal-born should at least *seem* reverent. Her lessons show — "

Taland interrupted wearily. "Biros, Clea is no different from your other students in her attitude, I'd wager. And actually, I do need her just now. We can discuss this later. I'm busy, as I've told you."

Taland reached to close the door, and Biros threw up his hand to stop it. Taland stared at him in disbelief. "The priesthood is more concerned than you know with irreverence." Biros snarled the word.

"Take care how you speak to me, Taland," he warned. "And as for that filthy boy . . ."

"Enough." For the first time Clea could remember Taland was furious and showing it. Her father raised his voice. "The boy is here because I want him here. And you'd better remember his name. It's Delos. Call him by it. He is not to be harried, Biros, by you or anyone else. Do you understand that clearly? He'll be helping me in the study and workroom."

Clea shot a look at Delos. He showed no surprise at her father's announcement. There was no need to — Biros showed enough surprise for all of them. His face was incredulous.

"But you have a man," the priest choked out. "You only need one. What of Marius?"

"What of him? He hasn't been satisfactory. Surely I can replace him?" Taland watched Biros closely. The priest began shaking his head, but Taland closed the door against him.

Clea's shoulders began to heave. The shock of Taland's strange fainting spell, the look on Biros's face as the door swung shut on him, added to the relief that her father was himself again, made her want to laugh. As she tried to stifle the urge, she heard her father address Delos, his voice diffident.

"Will you accept? Will you help me?" he asked. "It's best for you. You must believe me."

Delos hesitated. Then he spoke, softly, but Clea heard. Her laughter stopped suddenly.

"Who is Leo?" Delos demanded. "There are too many questions here. If I am to trust you enough to serve you, answer me this. Who is Leo?"

Chapter 4

The stone room rang with the intensity of Delos's question. Leo? Clea wasn't familiar with the name, but then nothing had been as usual today. But for a low harbor boy to question Taland — and that Taland tolerated it — was beyond Clea's imagining.

"I called you Leo?" Taland asked. "Did I, Clea?"

Clea thought her father had only tried to call her, but had been dazed. What difference did it make, anyway? If Delos wanted to ask anything, why didn't he ask about the golden mist? Surely it was more important.

"I don't know, Father," Clea said, realizing Taland was waiting for her answer. "You said something like that."

"It was Leo," Delos repeated.

Taland hesitated. Then he turned away to lean on the doorframe, his head bent in thought.

Suddenly Clea knew that her father was very tired. She noticed for the first time that his dark hair was streaked with silver. And then something incredible happened. She saw, or thought she saw, vast starry skies and gleaming globes about him. A great white pillar seemed to reach up enormously high, and beyond that a crystalline structure glittered, immense in the cold starlight.

A wave of sorrow washed over Clea. She gave a little cry and realized the illusion — if that's what it was — had disappeared. Her father looked across the now ordinary room to meet Clea's gaze and then swung to Delos.

"Where is it?" Delos cried. "That place. Oh, please." His hand was stretched toward Taland, his eyes wide. Why, Delos had seen it, too. Clea had thought the scene was in her mind.

Taland crossed to Delos. "You've given me two questions to answer," he said. "I'm sure, now, of your right to ask. But you may want to know more than you can digest at one time." He looked amused. "I know you don't understand me, but you will later. To answer your first concern, I'll tell you this. If I called you Leo, it was because you are much like him. Leo is my son, and for a moment I thought he was here. . . . It broke my concentration."

Clea was stunned. "But you . . . you have no son," she burst out. "Father, you don't. You know you don't. He would be my brother. I would know it." She was near tears.

Taland took Clea's hand. "You have an older brother, Clea," he told her. "His name is Leonis. Believe me, it wasn't my choice to keep it from you. And this isn't how I'd planned to tell you of it. I tried to convince the others that secrecy didn't have to go so far."

"Others?"

"I can't go into it now," Taland said. "I've said too much already. Like Delos, I'm too quick to act," he went on. "And after years of training, too."

Taland threw his arm over the harbor boy's shoulder. At that, the old one shrieked in alarm from where it had been dozing. It struck its tiny hands together furiously, and Taland laughed. But he never laughs, Clea thought, trying to make sense of it all.

"Tell your pet I mean you no harm," Taland said. "It will have to get used to us, won't it, if you accept my offer?"

"I'll come," Delos answered slowly. "No one would miss me down there. And I have answers to learn," he continued as if to himself. "Sir," he added guiltily, remembering the status of his new employer.

"Oh, yes, I'm sure you do," Taland agreed. He grinned, foolishly it seemed to Clea. "There's a small bedroom near mine, in the hall above the throne room," he went on. "I'll have a couch made up. You should be comfortable there. Later. . . . But first of all we'll think about clothing. And a bath." He measured Delos with a swift glance. "I'll lend you a drape until we have some made up for you. We're about the same size."

"He isn't my brother," Clea said loudly. "The servants sleep below the hill." Delos flushed, and Taland turned a disapproving look on Clea, who stared at the floor to avoid it.

"Daughter." Taland's voice was stern. "No more. Delos isn't a slave. If you can't welcome him, at least be civil." Then he continued more quietly, "I want his help, but I've asked for it, not ordered it. Delos is our guest."

Smoldering, Clea muttered feelingly under her breath.

"What did you say?" Taland lifted her chin.

Clea met his gaze. "Why is he our guest?" she cried. "We don't know him, and Granfer won't like his being here. He doesn't like strangers around." Red-faced, she went on. "Why is *he* so important? And where is my brother, if I really do have one? I'd rather have him here than Delos."

Clea wished she had never seen the harbor boy, and even more, that he would simply leave. She, who had always been first with her father, had been told that she was ignorant, that she wasn't an only child, and then been ignored for a nobody. Her eyes burned with angry tears.

Taland gave Clea's chin a rueful shake. "My dear child, don't you realize that Delos belongs here, with us? Why do you think you were led to bring him to me? Didn't you wonder what he said in that strange language when you first opened the door and found me?"

At that moment the world tilted. Clea pulled away from her father's grasp, then realized that the movement under her feet wasn't from her anger. As happened often in Atlantis, the earth itself had shifted. The movement came again, more strongly. Delos snatched up Boca to race for the door.

"Wait, Delos," Taland called after him over the clinking of jars in the herb room. "You needn't leave."

"Wait for the earthshaker?" Delos flung back. The sound of his running steps was hidden by a low rumble. The table clattered against the tiles as Clea followed her father into the little room. Together they moved the jars which were resting on the trembling shelves. By the time they reached the lower shelves the quake was over. Not a jar was broken.

"I'd almost perfected that ointment," Taland said, relieved. "I'd hate to have lost it. Thank you, Clea."

Clea had more important things on her mind. "Can you tell me where this mysterious brother of mine is?" she demanded. "Is there something wrong with him?"

"He's in Egypt, Clea, and perfectly healthy. Now don't bother asking again. I'll tell you more when I can." It was a rebuke. When Taland spoke in that tone, Clea knew to stop.

She stared up at the window slits where dust flecks danced in the sunlight. "Delos was afraid. He ran."

"Why not?" Taland replied. "Most people are afraid. I'll talk to him. Otherwise he'll waste time running outdoors every time we have a tremor. Don't misjudge him, though. He's no coward. He reacts on the basis of what he knows. There's no way he could know he's safe."

"How can I be safe when the earth shakes?" Delos challenged from the doorway.

"The time for disaster isn't here yet," Taland replied calmly, without looking up.

"How could you know?" Delos questioned. "No one knows these things. Did you learn it from — " He stopped, darting a suspicious glance at Taland.

Clea's father leaned forward, intent. "From?" he prompted.

"From the dead?" Delos blurted.

Taland burst into laughter. Delos scowled, but Clea was almost past thinking, she was so shocked.

Her quiet, purposeful father, laughing like a child? She couldn't believe it.

Taland moved into the workroom and dropped to the bench, still grinning. "All right, Delos, I won't laugh at you. But is that what you think? That I'm in touch with the dead?"

"I saw that golden mist." Delos threw the words at Taland, sullen. "You were . . . I could see *through* you. Clea?" He swung to face her and she nodded, feeling sick. The memory of her terror turned her fingers cold.

"You say you know the secrets of the earth-shaker," Delos continued. "What am I supposed to think? Where do you get your knowledge, if not from — "

Taland interrupted. "From a far place. From the place that held the language you spoke when you first saw me in the mist." He stood, watching the sky. "Do you remember?" he asked. Then Taland spoke the same unknown syllables Clea had heard Delos say. There was an odd turn of sound to the phrase, musical and soft-edged, and somehow ancient.

"I . . . I don't remember saying it," Delos stammered. "Sometimes. . . . Well, people say I do that once in a while. If I'm surprised, or in danger. But I never knew why, or what it meant. I didn't know it was a language." He went on slowly, as if talking to himself. "I used to think it might be a spell given to me at birth. But of course that couldn't be, could it? Who would bother?" His eyes were brilliant and lonely. Clea reached out to touch him, and he looked down at her hand.

"What do you mean?" Clea asked. "I don't understand what you're saying, Father."

Taland took a deep breath. "This is how I know Delos belongs here, with us," he said, choosing his words carefully. "This speech is older than the Citadel, older than you could imagine, and carefully kept secret. Delos couldn't have learned it. It comes from within." Taland spoke as if willing them to understand. "Some are born with it," he went on. "It came to me in my sixteenth year, a bit late."

Bewildered, Clea reached for Delos again. This time his hand gripped hers.

"You see?" Taland said. "Without knowing each other, you draw together." He looked again at the sky, and an emotion Clea couldn't identify crossed his face. The stark white sunlight fell from behind him. The silence in the room was like a living thing.

"Look at the star on your right palm, Clea," Taland told her. "Delos has one, too. 'By the blue space, nothing harm me.' That's what he said. He is Skyborn, Clea." Taland met her gaze. "And so are you."

Chapter 5

Clea looked at her right hand. The star at the base of her thumb, so deeply set that it looked more like a scar than a natural formation, jumped at her.

She had never paid attention to the mark. It was just part of her. Her eyes were dark, her hair black, she'd been born with an odd design in her palm, she was tall for an Atlantean girl of her age. . . . All equally unimportant, she'd thought. At least, until now.

Delos placed his hand by Clea's. An identical mark lay in his grimy palm, in the same place. Taland's hand was older — the fingers calloused and thickened by time — but the mark was there. "You see? The mark of the Skyborn," Taland said quietly.

"What does it mean?" Clea asked, bewildered.

"We're not like others," Taland said. "Our ancestors were not of this earth, but from beyond the stars. Can you both be satisfied with that much for a little longer? It will all be explained in due course, I promise you that."

"It can't be possible," Delos exclaimed. "Why are you saying this?"

"Because it's not only possible, it's true," Taland

assured him. "Remember the place you and Clea saw here, in this very room? It was the home of the Skyborn. You saw it from within . . . from your ancestral memories."

Clea stared at her father. "The vision was real?"

"Oh, yes," Taland said. "And it must remain secret, for reasons you'll learn. We carry a dangerous responsibility — "

Suddenly, a scream cut through the air. Without a word Taland ran into the hall in pursuit of running steps. Someone had broken in. There was a muffled shout from somewhere, then a scuffling noise. The scream was angry and continuous, and Clea realized it had come from Boca.

"What on earth?" Clea cried to an empty room, for Delos had disappeared, too. She rushed into the hall, following the sound of footsteps as the hall divided. When she took a left turn, Boca suddenly flew into her arms. It clung to her drape, chattering wildly.

"Oh, there," Clea soothed. The old one looked up at her with liquid eyes, head tilted, and she shivered. It had the face of an old, sad beggar. As if she'd offended it, it slid from her arms, tearing down the hall to find its master.

Clea watched Delos and her father come into view. So they didn't catch the intruder, she thought. Boca's screams must have chased him away.

"Any luck?" she called. Taland shook his head, frowning.

Clea knew why the palace was guarded. There had been violence before — once in her lifetime — but the back of the palace, the family's living area, had never been disturbed. "We'd better tell Grandfather about this," she said, thinking aloud.

Delos reached out to Boca, who clambered onto his shoulder. "Why is it important?" he asked. "The intruder is gone, so there's no danger. There may not have been any after all. Someone could have lost his way, and Boca frightened him."

"Only the family uses the back halls," Taland said. "Even the servants are rarely here. They come early in the morning, and then again to light the lamps before dark. We're quite cautious, I assure you."

"Because you could be harmed?" Delos swung Boca from his shoulder, smoothing the old one's fur. "The servants sleep below the hill, Clea said. Are you afraid of them, too?"

Taland stared at Delos. "By all above, boy, use your wits," he exclaimed. "There are treasures here, and secrets. They must be guarded. This is a different world than the one you know. We have to be careful." He rubbed his forehead, brooding.

Delos shrugged. "I've seen a man killed . . . for a pig," he said softly. "It wasn't even his pig. I've done without food rather than steal it and slept in doorways with the rats pulling at my sheet, when I had one. There's little I haven't seen, but I don't hide from the world as you do, here in the palace. They talk about it, down there." Delos shook his head and continued. "Isn't it better to face danger? Has Clea ever been among people, ordinary people? I doubt if she could survive."

"There are reasons, Delos, but certainly not the reasons you think." Taland's voice was equally quiet. He glanced at Clea, who was listening avidly. "Please go to my room to get a drape for Delos,

29

Clea. Then show him to the baths," he told her.

"The baths?" Clea's voice rose. "How can you talk about baths? What about the star in my hand, and in yours? You said we are Skyborn. Are you just going to leave it at that?" She had been sure Delos had gone too far, but Taland hadn't reacted as she'd expected. Instead, of getting angry he concerned himself with the harbor boy's comfort, ignoring Clea again.

"I don't expect this behavior from you, Clea," Taland said sharply. "I told both of you you'd have to wait for the full story. The intruder only stopped a discussion that was already over. I believe I asked you to show Delos to the baths."

"I don't think that's necessary," Delos said. "I need to get back to the harbor."

Taland stared at the boy. "You agreed to work with me," he said. "I want you living here."

"I understand that," Delos said. "But you seem to forget that I have obligations. I can't just move in. I've a couple of jobs to finish and rent to pay. Then I'll be back. But I'll be clean the next time I come up this hill." He gave Taland a level look. "You won't have to tell me to bathe."

"You are like Leo," Taland said. "Proud and stubborn."

"Among other things," Delos replied. "Do you still want me?"

"Oh, yes. Yes. Take your time," Taland murmured. He turned away and started down the hall, muttering, "So like Leo. Is it his age, or the times we live in?" Clea could still hear him muttering as he turned the corner.

"*Whee-oo.*" Delos let out an explosive breath,

flinging his arms wide. Boca leaped away with a shriek.

"What's wrong with you?" Clea cried. Delos had startled her, and she was in no mood for it. She didn't feel like herself. Her head ached, and even her body felt odd. She had wished for an end to boredom this morning, but that was before her familiar world had fallen apart. How could it be put back together?

"Who said anything was wrong?" Delos grinned. "Tell me, Clea, is it always like this here?"

"It was always calm until Boca came and brought his master," Clea snapped. She spun about and started away saying, "I don't care if you come back at all."

"But I will," Delos assured her.

Clea didn't bother to reply. She had asked for freedom and had been given nothing but mystery. If her father wouldn't tell her what she needed to know, perhaps she could get it out of the King, her grandfather. And as for Delos, he wasn't as important as her father seemed to think.

Six days later, Clea stood on the palace steps watching Delos climb the hill. Nothing had changed since he'd been there before. Clea's father and grandfather had spent a great deal of time together, but she hadn't been able to find out anything except that some sort of gathering was being planned. Forbidden to discuss any of it with Nera, Clea had waited impatiently for the harbor boy to come back. In the meantime, she went to classes as usual, until this morning, when Taland told her to wait for Delos.

"I'm supposed to show you around and then take you to the open court to meet with Father," Clea said when Delos reached her. "Come along. Are you staying this time?" She noticed he was scrubbed.

Delos shrugged. "For a while," he replied. "We'll see how it goes."

Clea led the way into a wide hall and took the stairs up. The tiled steps were done in a shell pattern. Delos stumbled, staring at the design, but Clea ran ahead. She reached the upper level and turned a corner, coming out on the balcony overlooking the throne room. "Father's rooms are here," she said. "Your room is two doors down."

Delos leaned in the doorway, watching Clea fling open a trunk at the foot of a narrow couch piled with pillows. She straightened, holding a cloth across her arm, which she handed to Delos. "I'll show you the baths. You could change there. Where's Boca?" she asked suddenly, looking about. The old one had disappeared.

Delos grinned. "Maybe he's afraid he'll have to take a bath," he said.

"It wouldn't hurt him," Clea said, moving toward the door. "He scratches. I hope his vermin don't scatter." Frowning, Delos followed her.

"The baths are here," Clea said as they reached the lower level. "I'll be on the north terrace." She pointed to the sunlit arch at the end of the hall. Delos gave a curt nod and left her.

She shrugged and ran to the terrace. So Delos was angry that she'd noticed Boca was dirty? She hadn't criticized Delos, after all. Anyway, it had nothing to do with her. Then she remembered what her father had said. *As close to you as your brother.*

But how could she be close to a brother she'd never seen? It's all so confusing, she thought, resentful.

With a sigh, Clea gazed at the mountains rising from the sea. She loved the terraces. They were her favorite refuge. There she could escape Nera's chatter and Biros's endless lectures and be alone to dream of far lands, of vast ships with painted sails, of hills slanting down to golden beaches.

A sea bird squawked rudely overhead. Clea yawned and rubbed her arm. The sun's warmth on her skin was pleasing after the chill of the palace. She wondered if Delos would take much longer, and stretched, turning her face up to the sky.

All at once angry sounds disturbed the peaceful morning. Clea ran to the wall and looked over. A blue-robed priest bent over Nera, holding her arm at a painful angle. Shocked, Clea leaned over the wall to see better. Nera tried to pull away. Her face was frightened. The priest growled something Clea couldn't hear, but the voice was unmistakably Biros's, and there was a threat in it.

"I don't know," Nera wailed. "Don't. . . . I tell you, I've never seen him before." She gasped and gave a thin, high cry.

Chapter 6

Furious, Clea leaned far over the wall. She opened her mouth to shout, but a hand covered it from behind and pulled her back from the scene. She saw Nera run, weeping, toward the side of the palace. Clea broke away to find Delos warning her to keep silent. He slipped to the wall without a sound, watched a moment, and then joined her.

"They've gone," he said.

"Didn't you see what Biros was doing?" Clea stormed. "Why did you stop me?"

"Sometimes it's better not to be seen," Delos replied. "What were they saying? Could you hear?"

"Biros hurt Nera's arm," Clea stammered, outraged. "He said something I couldn't hear, and then Nera said 'I don't know, I've never seen him before.' Something like that."

"Ah." Delos's eyes gleamed. "I see."

"And just what do you see?" Clea demanded.

Delos exhaled. "The big priest is really curious about me, isn't he?" He looked at Clea quizzically. "Interesting. Didn't you say your father's waiting for us? Come on." He disappeared into the palace, and she ran after him, frustrated.

Delos was nearly to the second turn in the main hall when Clea caught up with him. "You don't have to run," she panted. "You don't know where you're going anyway, so you have to wait for me."

Delos didn't slow his pace. "The open court? I've been there."

Surprised, Clea forgot her anger. "You've been there? When?" she questioned.

"Oh, some time ago," Delos remarked. "I saw your father there, and the King, of course. I know where the open court is. I wonder where Boca went," he mused. "You haven't seen him, have you?"

Clea didn't bother answering. "Why would you have come to court?" she pursued with a frown. "Surely not for a decision."

Delos stopped abruptly to scowl at her. "You really don't know very much, do you?" he asked.

"How dare you speak to me like that?" Clea snapped. "I know this much. Biros isn't allowed to hurt Nera, and you have no right to stop my shouting at him. I'm going to tell Father," she threatened.

"Oh, tell your father, of course. I expect you to," Delos said, waving a hand in a gesture that irritated her. "The open court days are for everyone, aren't they? Even a harbor rat can look at a King." He smoothed his hair, his mouth tense. "Do you know anything really practical, Clea?"

"You're the rudest person I've ever met, and I wish you had never come here," Clea cried.

Delos laughed. "But I did. I don't know why your

father wants me here, but I'm staying until I get some answers. We could try to be friends, you know."

Clea glowered fiercely. Delos grinned and turned away. Did he laugh? Clea was almost sure of it. She watched him go, and then followed. The meeting with her father was too important to miss. Perhaps he'd decided to tell them all about the Skyborn.

The two passed through the courtyard door and into the sunlight. Taland waited for them by the white stone chair the King used for the public meetings held there. He was plainly impatient. Clea picked her way across the squares. There were no flowers here, only dull black stones underfoot and the high sky and a queer silence disturbed by the sound of their footsteps.

The area was completely enclosed by towering palace walls except for a single wide metal gate, which glittered in the sun. Clea never came here alone. She didn't like the place at all. The stones on which she walked were as ancient as the mountains, the slaves said, much older than the palace which had been built around them. They whispered other tales of the stones, too. Tales which made Clea's skin creep.

Taland bowed low, touching both palms together. King Larok was entering the courtyard from the east, and Clea quickly followed her father's example. Delos ducked his head, too, and folded his hands. At least he knows how to behave in the King's presence, Clea thought grudgingly, and wondered at the same time why her grandfather was there.

"We're well met today," the King said. Clea

looked up to find him smiling at her. He was wearing a slender silver band and a simple robe, but even without ornate dress his dignity was impressive.

"I've missed you, Clea," he said. "Those messengers keep me so busy." His voice was regretful. "Are you well?"

"Oh, yes, Grandfather, quite well, but. . . ." Clea's anger returned in a rush, making her face hot. "You need to know this. It's Biros. Just now I saw him hurt Nera's arm. I was on the north terrace. He. . . ." In her haste she stumbled over her words. "Can't you punish him, Grandfather? He can't be allowed to do that."

"What?" Taland cried. "But we've no time for this now."

"Wait." The King looked at Clea, thoughtful. "Why did he do it?" he asked.

"Why, I . . . I don't know. Does it matter?" Clea replied, taken aback. "He hurt her, Granfer."

The King turned his attention to Delos. The sun beat down brilliantly in the courtyard. Clea felt odd, as if she stood apart, as if she were out of her body. She saw herself standing with the others by the throne, but at the edge of her vision an unknown throng wavered. There were no shining globes, no glittering walls such as she had seen in her father's study. There were only quiet figures standing together, as if in a dream. She shuddered, and the image broke. She was inside herself again, a bit dizzy, and the peopled shadows were gone.

Delos's eyes were wide. "It happened again. Who were they?" he demanded. His hands were tightly clenched at his sides.

"Why, your people, and ours," the King replied courteously. There was a faint gleam in his gaze.

"But Biros . . . what of him?" Clea burst out, shaken.

"We know our enemies, Clea." King Larok's broad face creased in a grim smile. "However, Biros will have to wait. You've been called here for something much more important. Would you sit? Please, all of you." Clea sank to a nearby bench with Delos, and Taland settled to a stone below the King's chair.

Larok rubbed his hands together. "My son tells me we've found an unknown Skyborn," he said cheerfully. "Welcome, Delos." Delos bowed gravely, his eyes guarded. So he has come to greet Delos, Clea thought. She hoped her grandfather wouldn't be as foolish about Delos as her father was.

"Clea," the King said, turning to her, "your father and I feel it's time for you to be fully informed of your heritage. In fact, child, you seem to have insisted upon it." He fell silent and Clea fidgeted, waiting. At last he spoke again. "So. These . . . have joined to witness." He gestured broadly at the courtyard behind them.

Startled, Clea turned around, but no one was there. The courtyard was empty, except for the four of them. Could he mean the shadows she'd thought she'd seen were real people? Then where were they? Disturbed, she looked back at her grandfather as he continued.

"By his appearance, Delos has forced us to move up the date of this gathering. We have consulted and have decided it's our responsibility to hold the ceremony now, for both of you."

Clea looked away, apprehensive. Would she have

to go among those wavering shadows?

"You know I'd let nothing harm you," her grandfather said gently. "Clea, will you agree to the ceremony?" She nodded, her heart pounding. "And Delos?" the King asked.

Delos caught his lip in his teeth. "Sir, I am a stranger. How can I agree to something I don't know anything about?"

Larok smiled. "You only have to listen, Delos. You needn't do anything. I can give you the same assurance I gave Clea. After the telling, you'll be asked if you accept your destiny, and that's all."

"If I say no?" Delos asked.

"I think you'll find you won't be able to do that." The King's voice was soft. "Our people are ready. Will you stay?"

Our people. Clea's head turned again. The figures now formed a semicircle closer behind her. They were not more than thirty steps away. The figures were more clearly defined this time. Oh, I know, Clea thought in surprise. It's like looking at someone's reflection in a pool, and not at the person at all. She had no sense of fear. It was as if this way of seeing were perfectly normal.

"Do you know them to be there?" the King asked.

"Yes, I see them, Grandfather," Clea replied, wondering why he asked.

"And you, Delos?" The King watched him closely.

"Yes, sir." Delos's voice was steady. He paused and then blurted out, "I'll stay."

Clea knew Delos was afraid. *Father won't let anything happen to us*, she sent before she remembered Delos couldn't hear her.

King Larok stood and slowly raised his right hand

high. The members of the gathering responded with the same gesture. There were both men and women in the group, some very old, but no children. A few of the faces seemed strangely familiar. Though the outlines of the figures shimmered, they were as real as . . . as Nera, or herself. But how could they be? Her grandfather's voice was solemn, and she listened carefully.

"By the blue space and in the presence of the Ageless God and our people, know that the choosing of my dear granddaughter, Clea. . . ." The King's voice roughened and he stopped to clear his throat. Clea felt close to tears at the affection he showed so openly. "And of the Skyborn, Delos," the King went on more strongly, "in whose finding we rejoice, is at hand.

"Because the mark we carry is both an honor and a burden, the history of our people must now be retold, for it is on this basis that the Skyborn have always chosen. These two must decide to accept or deny the destiny of we who watch, but dare not interfere. Who guide, but pledge to wait."

Clea edged closer to Delos, her mouth dry. Her grandfather smiled slightly in reassurance and began.

"Eight thousand turns about this sun have passed," he said, his gaze distant, "since we fell from the sky. . . ."

Chapter 7

"So wrote Tana, the scribe of the first down, and Nika after her, and Pol the poet, and these words are their words, and I speak these words for them, and all those after them, and those that are to come." The King's voice was strong and deep, and the shadowy throng drew closer to hear. The King began. . . .

The starship *Longspeed*, chartered by the Federation of Allied Planetary Research, cruised toward her destination at warp six steady. Directed by the ship's CBR6N, she held her course toward a distant galaxy, and the crew relaxed, joking over miktar in the ready room.

Com Ranson stood by the porthole, brooding as he stared out into the velvet of deep space. He missed his family and resented being there. Oh, he knew the run was necessary — a disastrous explosion on Obral had damaged the city's dome severely, and materials had to be sent, and quickly — but he was due a twelveday break between runs, and there hadn't been time to take any of it. Lessa had understood, of course, but she had been disappointed. And the children had been asleep, so he hadn't even been able to see them.

Karn, the ship's engineer, abruptly appeared at Ranson's side. Worry was written on her face. "Power source dimming, sir," she said softly.

Without a word Ranson set down his mug. It cracked with the force of his movement. With Karn following, he threaded his way through the noisy tables and made for the bridge, where gleaming green and amber lights ran across the primary panel. He looked at the engineer.

"The panel is normal," Ranson said, puzzled. Then he caught the direction of Karn's eyes and whirled to see a rank of lights flicker to red, then amber, and back to red. It was impossible, yet the evidence was before him. He began verification with the Cyber, coding questions rapidly as answers flashed.

"How could this happen?" Ranson shot at Karn. She shrugged, her eyes desperate.

"We were sent out again too soon," she said. "It might not have been caught anyway, sir."

He pushed away from the console. "The warp's gone. We're at conventional speed. Cyber says there's little time. Make sure the power room's secured and join us in the bay as soon as you've finished." She was running before he'd stopped speaking.

Ranson alerted the crew. "By my order, all hands to the bay. Haste. Ranson." He thought a moment and pulled his communicator from his belt, flipping it on as he brought it to his lips. "Char, come to the bridge alone, at once. Ranson."

He hadn't long to wait. When his first officer burst onto the bridge, he ordered a course set for the nearest safe planet. "We must have enough oxygen," he warned. "And pray there's time to get there," he muttered to himself, his jaw set. Char wasted no time. His long fingers were already busy at his station, comparing different planets, rejecting one, going immediately to the next. Ranson left him.

There were thirty-two aboard the *Longspeed*. Ranson found them in the bay and told them. He spoke soberly of cooperation. It meant life or death after landfall, he said, a point nobody debated. He didn't have to tell them what would happen if the power source imploded before they landed. They knew.

Everything portable had been pulled down and placed by the exit hatches by the time the ship jerkily settled to land. The Cyber was left behind, its functions useless without power. They were marooned between mapped space, on the edge of an unfamiliar pinwheel galaxy, with all contact to the Federation gone.

The crew jumped onto land to find themselves in warm, muggy air, not too different from their own. They'd landed on a small pleasant island, but there was no time to look at the lush terrain. Danger worried them. Running, they carried the gear through a gap in the low hills.

They were fortunate. The *Longspeed* waited to destruct until they were safe. It took half the island with it in a thundering roar of flame. The sea was bloody in the flaring light, and the crew stood in silence, each thinking of home.

"I couldn't get a message through, sir," Char said, echoing the crew's thoughts.

"They'll look for us." Ranson's voice was steady,

his mind already busy with plans. "And we'll make sure we're seen when they do." His sharp eyes caught a movement in the shadow of the trees, and he held up a hand to alert the others, loosening the weapon at his belt.

The King paused in his recital, his eyes closed, and Clea drew a faint shuddering breath. She couldn't understand some of the things her grandfather had said, but it scarcely mattered, she was so caught up in the tale. It seemed she could see Ranson moving toward danger on the dark island as the tense crew waited, though she heard Granfer's voice clearly through the scene. The silence in the courtyard was immense. The King opened his eyes, and went on.

The primitive people native to the islands saw the destruction of the starship and fell to the ground in fear. They prayed to their gods to save them from the terrible high flame. When the sound died, the braver among them crept to the shores to whisper together. The gods must be there, they said, staring toward the dying fires of the torn island.

Fear made them quick. They gathered the best of their succulent fruit, and a whole roast animal, meant for a feast, and went into a crude boat with the harvest. A young girl, oiled and painted, was pushed in beside the offerings. She wept as the natives pushed the boat across the narrow waters, and she had to be carried onshore and through the trees.

Ranson went to meet them. It wasn't a new experience for him — the scene had been repeated on other young planets — but there had always been a starship to take him away again. Now there was none, and it was an important meeting. It could be a very long time before they were found, he thought somberly.

The Commander showed pleasure at the gifts of food, and by a sign carefully refused the live sacrifice. He removed a bracelet Lessa had given him and presented it to the leader, who accepted the gift with awe. At last the natives backed away, heads bowed, to melt into the night.

"We'll begin building tomorrow," Ranson told the crew. They were sprawled on the grass, eating. A wood fire flickered. "With the gear we were taking to Obral, we can put together a solid place." The crew was silent, but the Commander saw Char's face flinch, and motioned him to speak.

"Sir, I'm not so much worried about a place to stay as I am about being found," the first officer said slowly. "I don't think we have a chance of rescue if we can't signal. . . ."

"Yes. But, Char, there are more ways to signal than by computer," Ranson replied, cheerful. "Pyramids, remember? The old ways. Not as efficient, but . . . And if we build our quarters mathematically, completely unlike anything these people could create, and make them enormous — "

"Why, we'd be living in a beacon." Char looked immensely relieved, and Ranson grinned, noting a general brightening of faces. He knew if they could keep busy, and if they had even a distant hope, the unit would survive. It was his responsibility to the Federation to see that it did. It might take years, maybe centuries. . . . I'll never see Lessa again, he thought bleakly, yet unsurprised. He had long ago accepted that his life would end like this, on a planet not his own. It had shadowed his deepest happiness.

"We'll call this planet Earth," Ranson said abruptly. "In honor of our own. It will, after all, be Earth to us until we get home."

Clea moved involuntarily, shocked. Another, older, Earth? Was that what she had seen in the workroom? Suddenly she realized that she was involved, indeed, was herself a part of the story. Her grandfather was speaking the history of her people, her own ancestors. The King's voice changed, darkened, yet pride rang in his measured words as he continued.

They used the tools they had saved from the starship to build as the natives watched. The work went quickly. Yet, caught up in this great effort, the Skyborn forgot their primary rule, that the natives of any planet they touched should not be confronted with advanced technology. And so mighty gates soon rose while vast pyramids lifted splendidly above the jungle growth. They trapped the sun within the stones and were not slowed by darkness. A laboratory was installed, and cataloging of the environment begun. The mapping of the planet was planned, and all went well.

Then the natives began to gather before the high walls. Ranson shrugged it away, busy with his work. They were short of writing materials; could they make more? And the gardens took too much time, perhaps growing tanks could be improvised. He frowned and took himself to the laboratory to debate. If the Skyborn had only heeded the signs.

The blow came in the night, when the wind lay breathless in the warm, moist air. They were attacked in their sleep, within the safety of their own force-lit walls. They were too different and had not concealed their difference, had not remembered. Evil, the natives chanted as the knives rose and fell. Evil are these gods. Slay the earth-changers. *Ai-ah-nam-ah-ana.* And blood ran over the black stones.

Four men and three women, escaped into the night. They lay in the thick vines, watching as the bodies of their friends were thrown down from the terraces. The natives, having no way to count, were satisfied they had killed all the intruders and began to smash equipment with their clubs. At last they stopped. It was dawn.

When the seven who had been spared could enter the courts safely, there was only a little equipment left. They found a crude boat to load it in, and left the islands to the slow green vengeance of the jungle, pushing off into the rising sun. They would survive, they swore. By the blue space, they would build again. They would grow and colonize. They would study and document, as they had been trained to do, and place their signs for old Earth to find. The small boat rolled in the heavy sea as they took oaths to live at peace with this planet and to help only in ways that would not again be misunderstood.

A great storm blew them south, and as it died a child was born in the bottom of the clumsy craft, a strong squalling boy. He was the first of the Skyborn to come into life on this new Earth, his hand marked with the star. He who would be called Ahki, the Gifted One, was barely an hour old when the boat touched a narrow strip of shore. The mountainous jungles of the land we know as Peru rose above it, the cradle of the colonies of the Skyborn.

They settled there and remembered, and it was there that Ahki directed that the signs to guide the starships be laid on the great dry plain. It took a very long time. They sent colonists overland to a hot, wet place of mighty storms and raised their mark there, in the land of the Yucatan. Then on by sail to Kemet — to Egypt — and the terrible work of the pyramids, and time continued to pace, and the Skyborn continued to be faithful.

In their loneliness they carved vast forms and statues, placing them in forgotten places, in memory of their lost world. And their knowledge grew as they worked toward the day when they would be exiled no longer. Oh, beautiful planet, blueveined against the sky, how they loved her. . . . But she was not their own.

The courtyard shone with the grandeur of memory. Clea sat entranced, dreaming of mighty works, and Delos coughed to cover his emotion.

"This, then, is your heritage," the King said quietly. "You have been told here, on the black stones of another time. Clea, Delos, this is your future if you accept it. Atlantis is young, the work is yet to be completed, and there is even more elsewhere. The choice is yours. And it must be made."

Chapter 8

Clea rubbed her eyes. Taland stood beside her, touching her shoulder lightly. "Is it too much for you all at once, Clea?" he asked. "You're supposed to decide now, but you can take a little time to think about it. It's a serious decision."

Clea raised her head proudly and stood. "I'm ready now, Father," she said. Then she turned to face the King. "Our people need my loyalty," she went on, knowing there was no other choice she could make. She felt much older than when she had wakened that morning. "I claim the Skyborn."

"And so do I, gladly." Delos spoke at her shoulder, his voice shaken. "To have a people . . ." He fell silent, his eyes glowing.

The King raised his arms. "Now all these present know that we are one in the rhythm of the universe." His words rang across the courtyard. "You may greet your own," he cried. The glimmering figures pressed closer, smiling in welcome. One, a tall woman with dark hair wound about her head, held out her hands to them in a joyful gesture.

"That's your mother, Clea," Taland said. "How proud you've made her."

"These are the dead, then?" Clea asked, strangely calm. The figures wavered as she watched, breaking into dancing silver particles that faded slowly into the air. The courtyard held only the four of them again, and she sighed.

"No, Clea." Taland's face was twisted and his voice uneven. "None of these are dead. They're Skyborn, like us. They sent their force to witness your joining, but their bodies remained in their own lands. We can see and hear each other this way, but we can't touch. Not anymore. We've lost that ability, along with other things."

Clea stared at her father. "My mother is alive?"

Taland nodded. "She's with Leo, in Egypt. When the call came for Phrene, you were a baby. She took Leo with her, and left you with me. She's a scribe, a recorder of history. She was needed there." Taland looked away. "I couldn't tell you that, Clea. Not until now. Sometimes children repeat things that are dangerous. Remember Ranson. The danger is always there for Skyborn."

Clea noted absently that Delos stood in earnest conversation with the King. She felt detached and light, as if she could float away like a fluff of seed, part of the wholeness of earth and sea and sky. Only think, I have a mother, she thought, remembering the smiling image. She wondered why she had ever thought the courtyard was a fearful place. She was only half-listening as Taland continued to speak.

"I hope you can forgive me for keeping this from you," Taland was saying. "Your brother hasn't been gathered yet — hasn't been offered the ceremony of decision — so he doesn't know you or I exist. It will be hard for him, too, when he does know. But

I miss them both, very much. And your mother misses you."

How odd, Clea thought. How could her father possibly think she didn't understand? What is different is feared, and what is feared is destroyed. The Skyborn were different. The difference must be hidden. As a child, she might have betrayed them all. . . . She knew, now, why she had been kept away from the world.

"Have you been worrying all this time that I might not forgive you?" Clea asked. "But there was no choice. It's something you and my mother had to do. If I'm old enough for the gathering, don't you think I can understand why we have to be so careful?" We, she thought proudly. I, too — "I, too," she said aloud, "am Skyborn, after all."

A fierce chattering made Clea jump. Then she burst into laughter. Boca was back, scolding Delos loudly. His long tail trembled with intensity.

"What have you done to anger your friend?" the King asked, laughing.

Embarrassed, Delos pulled the little fingers from his hair. "I forgot to feed him. He takes it very badly. He has no patience, sir," he said.

Taland groaned. "Delos, forgive me. It's well past midday, and I completely forgot about food."

"Don't beat yourself about it, it wastes time," the King chided. "It would be more sensible if you simply fed these two and the animal. It's foolish to let Skyborn die of hunger in a time of plenty." His eyes twinkled.

Chagrined, Taland agreed. Can't he tell Grandfather is joking? Clea wondered, and wondered too why her father was always so serious. Yet he laughed at Delos, she remembered, resentful.

Phrene would not have forgotten to feed her daughter. Startled, Clea realized she had heard her father's thought. It was the first time she had heard anything other than a direct message to herself.

Clea dropped her head to hide behind a curtain of hair. Somehow she felt guilty and disturbed at the sadness in his thought. It was uncomfortable to see her father as a person with concerns like her own, and learn that he was unhappy. Pity swelled in her chest.

"Come, we have work to do, Taland," the King said. "Clea, don't you think you could all survive on candlefruit until dinner? This creature should be fond of it. Run along to the kitchens. Your father and I need to decide on your training as new Skyborn."

Stung at being sent away so abruptly — she was Skyborn, after all — Clea bowed and left the court-yard. Delos followed, and Boca trailed behind. There were many things Clea would have asked the King, but they could wait. She ran through the short hall at the rear of the palace and down the narrow dirt path to the kitchens.

The kitchen slaves watched in silence as Clea pulled off a slender section of candlefruit to give to Boca. The creature peeled it with astonishing speed, stuffed it down, and reached for another. Clea took sections for herself and Delos and handed the stalk to a servant. Soon the workers were nudging each other, grinning to see the old one grabbing for more.

Clea watched Boca without seeing him and turned to walk across the dusty yard alone. She sank to a stone outcropping to frown at the distant mountains, her half-eaten candlefruit dangling forgotten from her hand.

"Something on your mind?" Delos asked, dropping down beside her.

"Pyramids." Clea threw her fruit down the slope toward the water and drew her knees up, hugging them. "Delos, when you told me Boca came from the place of high pyramids, did you mean Egypt? Remember, Granfer said Skyborn built those?" She flushed. "I didn't know there were pyramids in Egypt. I just knew that's where we buy much of our cloth." She spread out a fold of her drape, finely woven, and looked at it.

"There are things you know that I don't know," Delos said quickly. "Everyone has to learn."

Clea waved a hand to dismiss the subject. "In the baths," she went on, "there's a small pyramid. Did you see it? It's about two hands tall?" She placed her hands to show him the size. "It's used for keeping the scraping knives sharp, so they don't have to be ground on the stone."

"I saw it, but I didn't know it sharpened. I did wonder why it was there," Delos said. "How does it work?"

Clea shrugged. "They put the blades inside it, and they don't grow dull. But, Delos, Granfer said pyramids were beacons, signals — the big pyramids, I mean. How can pyramids sharpen blades and be beacons, too?"

"Your father never told you that? Of course, he might not know," Delos said. "If it's been eight thousand turns since we got here, there's probably much that's been forgotten."

Delos reached for a stick and drew it idly across the dust at his feet, tracing a triangle. He stared at it, and then drew lines up from the apex, fanning them out to form an upside-down triangle without a base, resting tip to tip with the first one. Clea shifted impatiently.

"Look, Clea." Delos jabbed eagerly at the upper triangle with his stick. "If some sort of force could be concentrated there . . . If it could be drawn out of the sky, wouldn't the loss of that force as it was pulled down be noticed?"

"I don't know what you're talking about," Clea told him, now bored. "If you don't know how pyramids can be beacons, why not admit it?"

"Come on, Clea," Delos argued. "Think. A pyramid can't sharpen blades by itself, can it? Nothing like that happens in ordinary buildings, and the same stone is used in each. There must be something we don't know about, some principle that explains it. There's a power brought in through that shape." He looked awed by the idea.

"You don't know that," Clea said, scoffing. "It's just something you imagine might be so." She waved a humming cloud of insects away, watching them settle on her discarded fruit.

"Well, somebody has to imagine it for the first time," Delos cried. "And if the secret's lost, somebody has to think of it again." He glowered at her.

"So?" Clea shot back. She couldn't think of anything else to say.

Delos jumped to his feet. "I'm going back to the palace," he said. "Maybe your father will be in his workroom now. I'd like to talk to him about this. After all, he searches for answers, even if you don't." He dashed away, his jaw set.

"What of your precious Boca?" Clea shouted. The slaves stood watching her, and she was infuriated that Delos should embarrass her before the servants.

"Bring him yourself," he tossed back. "I have other things to do."

With as much dignity as she could manage, Clea rose to retrieve Boca, whose stomach bulged like a drum. "Your master is impossible," she scolded, giving the creature a little shake.

Clea, bring Delos to my study. I'd like to talk to both of you before we dine tonight, Taland sent. *There's much to discuss before we start your new training.*

Clea started for the palace, her cheeks hot. *He's already on his way,* she sent.

There was a silence. *Ah. He is eager. Good,* Taland sent. *Come along, Clea.*

He's no more eager than I, Clea thought, feeling again the thrill of adventure that had shaken her at the gathering. She quickened her pace. *Coming, Father. Wait for me.*

Chapter 9

Clea had never worked so hard in her life. With the exception of two days when the King had sent for Taland, she and Delos had studied unceasingly. Now, a month past the gathering, her head spun with blocks of information unlike anything she'd learned in six years of temple classes. She began to see all that had been lost to the Skyborn, and, like Delos, was hungry for any bits of knowledge available. Perhaps Skyborn secrets could be rediscovered after all.

The King had summoned Biros immediately after the gathering, both to reprimand him and to warn against any harm to Nera. The priest hadn't taken it well. Nor was Biros pleased that Clea no longer came to the temple. He'd argued with Taland over it, but Taland waved him away.

Clea was surprised to find she missed Nera's company more than she'd expected, though they still shared their meals. But Taland's store of scrolls and fragments drew her more strongly each day. It could hold the key to the future of her people, and Clea was determined to learn all she could.

Delos was equally determined. When Taland

demonstrated how he charted earth's surges and tremors, the boy was enchanted. He announced he, too, would become a planetologist, and measure earth and sky. Clea thought her gift might be as a recorder, but as Taland said, basic knowledge should come first.

One morning Clea entered the workroom as usual only to find that Taland was again required in the King's chamber. With the day free, Delos went off to explore the vineyards, and Clea took Boca with her to walk in the sacred grove before the temple. She brought fruit along to share with the old one and laughed at his antics.

Refreshed by the sweet cool air of the grove, Clea had started back to the palace, when she heard a hiss. She froze and looked down, expecting to see a snake. Instead, a figure slipped from behind the fig trees. It was Nera, her face blotchy from crying.

"Oh, Clea," Nera whispered. "I thought you'd never come. I waited and waited. . . ." And with that, she began to shake, clapping both hands over her mouth.

"Wait, Nera, don't weep," Clea begged, shocked. Boca squirmed free and jumped into the shadows, its eyes gleaming in the fig leaves. Nera began to sob noisily. Perplexed, Clea tried again.

"Nera, if you don't stop, you won't be able to talk," she reasoned. "And if you can't talk, how can you tell me what's wrong? Is it Biros again, the beast? Has he hurt you?"

"It's not that," Nera managed to say, shaking her head.

"Well, what then?" Clea asked, beginning to be annoyed. Then she saw the fear in Nera's eyes. Her own narrowed. Nera wanted to tell her something, but was afraid to say it.

Clea scowled, trying to understand, and then across her inner vision a picture flickered, a picture of Nera and . . . a priest? Ah, and handsome, too. The picture faded quickly, and Clea caught her breath. She remembered seeing old Earth in her father's thoughts, but they'd used mind-speech together for a long time. Could it be possible that she could see Nera's thoughts as well? Excited past caution, she leaped out mentally and turned her sight inward.

Clea saw Nera staring at the young priest. They stood in the temple classroom with the stone door shut behind them. The edges of the room were obscured by mist, but Clea could see their faces clearly. The priest nodded forcefully, as if assuring Nera of something. A lock of pale hair fell across his brow. He looked worried. Clea remembered him now. He was new at the Citadel.

Clea watched Nera shake her head. *No. I won't listen. It can't be true.* Fear and confusion crept into her eyes.

You must believe me. I know, the priest said. Nera's face crumpled in distress, and he pulled her into his arms. *Tell her, can't you? You must. You can talk to the girl. Tell her of the danger*, he said. He smoothed Nera's curls, bending to her.

Embarrassed, Clea let the picture go. Her vision cleared rapidly as the image faded. While Nera's tears had dried on her face, she was quite pale. Clea thought quickly. She couldn't tell Nera what she knew, but she had to discover what the priest's warning meant. There was no doubt in Clea's mind that she, herself, was the one the warning was meant for.

She tried to look reassuring. "If you want me to know what you're so upset about, Nera, you'd better just tell me," she said.

"It's . . ." Nera hesitated and swallowed, looking toward the west wall of the temple. Clea looked, too, but there was no one about, only grass and shrub and trees in the morning light. The breeze had fallen, and the leaves hung idle on their branches. Nothing moved. Clea turned back to Nera.

"It's Biros," Nera said, her words falling out in a rush. "He's trying to get the other priests to. . . ." She stopped biting her lip and took a deep breath.

"Well, what is it?" Clea demanded.

"Biros says you're evil, all of you. It's something about the courtyard and your father's workroom. I don't understand it," Nera said, "but he thinks you should be removed, even the King. Taken from the palace. Biros wants to — " She stopped abruptly.

"Biros wants to rule Atlantis." Clea couldn't believe it, but that had to be what Nera meant. Nera nodded. "What makes him think he could do that?" Clea cried, furious. "And how do you know?" she added hastily.

"Bellini told me," Nera said, blushing. "The new priest. We're friends. He doesn't agree with Biros, but he may be the only one who doesn't."

Clea stared at her, hoping this was all a mistake. "Evil," Biros had said. Clea remembered Ranson's fate so many centuries ago and shivered. She disliked Biros, but she couldn't believe he'd be insane enough to plot against the King. Everyone knew Larok's power. This couldn't be happening. "How can you tell me this?" Clea cried, hardly knowing what to think.

Nera drew herself up. "I know where my loyalty belongs," she said stiffly. "Do you think I can forget what your father has done for my family? I was thin when I first came to the Citadel, remember? My own brothers would be begging for food in the streets . . . or worse . . . if I hadn't been chosen to be your companion." Bright color burned in her cheeks.

Clea looked away. Of course she knew Nera's background. She was simply so used to Nera that she had fallen into the habit of snapping at her — mostly because Nera could leave the Citadel when she chose, and Clea couldn't. Yet Nera has her own dignity, she thought, ashamed.

"Nera," Clea said, and then hesitated. What could she say? "I'm . . . sorry," she went on, putting her hand on Nera's plump arm. "I really am."

"It's nothing," Nera said with a deprecating gesture, but Clea could tell she was pleased with her apology. "What are you going to do, Clea?" Nera asked.

"Let's go to my room and talk about it," Clea said. "I don't think we should discuss it here."

Clea looked around for Boca, trying to sort out what she'd heard. She still didn't think Biros could harm her grandfather, but the fact that he wanted to disturbed her. First she'd hear all Nera could tell her, and then she'd tell the King. She remembered his saying "We know our enemies." It reassured her. Surely things weren't as bad as Nera seemed to think.

Boca was nowhere in sight. Clea shrugged, then pulled open the door, and began walking quickly down the hall ahead of Nera. To make sure no one noticed the two of them, she placed her sandals as quietly as possible on the tiles. She also listened for other sounds. Clea found she couldn't look at the thin gold masks that hung on the walls as she passed. Their great staring eyes and thin-lipped smiles only added to the uneasy feeling in her chest.

"Why the hurry?" Nera puffed, trying to keep up. "Rushing won't change anything. And Biros can't do anything right now, anyway. He's teaching class. I told him I was sick to get out of it." She stopped to fan herself.

"Hush," Clea hissed. She grabbed Nera's arm. Heavy footsteps were coming toward them. Nera froze. *Biros.* Her lips formed the word without making a sound. In terror, she jerked open the door beside them and darted through it.

Taken by surprise, Clea stood still. The door shut just as Biros turned the corner twenty steps away. He stopped, and then walked purposefully toward her.

"Clea." The priest's voice was flat. It was apparent he hadn't expected to see her there. It was obvious to Clea, too, that he was hiding his anger.

Two can play that game, Clea thought. She tilted her head slightly. For the first time she was grateful to her father for making her practice self-control ever since she was small.

Biros reached Clea and stopped. His deep-set eyes watched her coldly. She returned the look without moving.

"It's odd to find you here at this time of day," Biros said. He pushed his head forward as he spoke, a menacing movement which gave his words darker meaning. Then he looked up and down the hall to see if Clea was alone. Suddenly she was glad Nera was close by, even though they would be no match for Biros. He can be a dangerous man, Clea thought. Her body tightened.

"But why are you here, Biros?" Clea asked. "Isn't it time for class? You will be missed." She saw his eyes flicker and knew he was considering her reply, and more, her tone of voice.

"You have been removed from my classes," the priest said slowly, as if feeling his way. "You and that harbor boy are with your father daily. It's not seemly — "

"It is the King's wish, Biros," Clea interrupted. "Are you criticizing his decisions?" Contempt edged her words. "This palace is my home. The hall in which we stand is mine. And if I am to be spied upon and my movements judged by you, perhaps my grandfather will want to know why. Are you prepared to tell him?" Clea challenged, too angry now to be cautious.

"There is much an ignorant girl like you could learn. Perhaps even respect for those more powerful than yourself," Biros snarled, his face mottled with rage. Clea gasped at the insult, but she wasn't prepared for what happened next. All at once Biros held her arm in a hard grip, pinching her flesh.

"From where does this Delos really come?" the

priest questioned, his breath hot on Clea's face. "And with what message, for what purpose?"

Clea stared up at Biros. He twisted her arm cruelly and then suddenly released her, raising his fist as if to strike an answer from her.

Clea drew herself up tall. Alien words fell from her lips. "You. Worshiper of false gods. By the blue space, you dare not harm me, for I am not alone," she shouted. She knew she'd spoken in the old tongue, the language of the Skyborn. There was no time to wonder how it could have happened, only to regret that it had. Biros drew back as if he had been struck. His face was alive with triumph.

"So I was right," he muttered, his voice thick. It dropped to a whisper. "Now we shall see." And he whirled and was gone, leaving Clea shaken.

Clea stood alone in the hall. She remembered having said proudly to her grandfather, "I claim the Skyborn." She had thought then of the glory of belonging to the great venture, and of the heart-stopping hope that the starships would come soon. She was aware now that being Skyborn meant many things, and indeed, could be dangerous. How could she not have realized it before? She hugged her arms tightly to stop shivering.

Chapter 10

Clea turned abruptly to open the door behind her.

"Nera? He's gone. Come on out," she called, peering into the clutter. The room was used for storing jars fresh from the kilns, and they were everywhere, stacked nearly to the ceiling.

Nera crawled from behind a huge black-banded jar. Her eyes glinted white in the gloom, and her clothing was covered with red dust.

"You couldn't be more messy if you had hidden inside the jar," Clea told her as Nera attempted to brush herself off. "Why did you leave me?"

"I didn't," Nera protested. "Wouldn't you have needed me to go for help if there was trouble? Did Biros frighten you?" Her face puckered in belated concern.

"I'm not afraid of Biros," Clea scoffed, but she knew she had almost goaded him into striking her.

"Clea?" Delos appeared so suddenly that Clea jumped. She spun to face him. His sandals hung about his neck, leaving him barefoot. No wonder she hadn't heard him coming.

"Don't do that," Clea cried, disturbed that Delos could so easily slip up on her. What if he had been Biros coming back?

Delos waved impatiently. "Has anyone passed through here?" he demanded. Nera nodded. "Who, then?" he asked urgently. "Did you recognize him? Who was it? Have you lost your tongues?"

"No one's been here but Biros," Clea said. "Why?"

Delos scowled. "Is that priest everywhere?" he asked. "Surely he wouldn't have — "

"We've quite enough mystery without your making more," Clea told him. "I've just had a talk with Biros. He seems to think you're dangerous, did you know that?"

"What on earth do you mean?" Delos asked.

"I've noticed something about you, Delos," Clea said. "You always have questions, but no answers. Just once I'd like an answer. Biros asked me from where you came, and with what message. Why is he so worried about you?"

"Why, Biros asked me that, too," Nera put in. "When he hurt my arm that time. But I didn't know what he meant. Do you, Clea?"

"Perhaps Delos knows," Clea said. "I remember saying it was peaceful here until he arrived."

"And quite boring, too, remember?" Delos flared. "Don't accuse me, Clea. You know as well as I that we're both — "

Skyborn. The unsaid word trembled between them. Horrified, Clea interrupted loudly. "Enough of this nonsense. Can you tell me why you're chasing Biros?" She threw a warning look at Delos. He was right to remind her of their bond, but not now, not in front of Nera.

Delos flushed. "It may not have been Biros who did it, of course," he said, "but someone's been in your father's workroom, Clea. It's been ransacked. When I left the vineyards, I went to see if your father had come back. The door to the workroom was wide open."

Clea was astonished. "But it's always locked. Father will be furious. Was anything taken? You don't suppose Biros — "

"I don't know," Delos said. "There's no one else in the halls, and Biros was here. Shouldn't he be at the temple?"

"Of course," Clea replied. "I can't believe he left his class. But I do know he was angry. It was obvious." Nera, frightened again, began to sniffle.

"Oh, Nera, stop that," Clea snapped at her.

"What's wrong?" Delos asked in surprise.

"Nera's upset because she thinks she's uncovered a plot," Clea replied. "She thinks Biros wants my grandfather's crown."

"What?" Delos exclaimed.

Clea pushed her hair back from her face. "Everything happens at once, doesn't it?" she went on. "Father's workroom searched and rumors of a plot to take the throne. The only thing I'm sure of is that Biros is suspicious of you, Delos."

Nera stopped wiping her nose to stare at Clea. "How can you say that after what I've told you?"

Clea lifted her chin. "Look, Marius could have torn up Father's rooms to get even for being dismissed. And as for Bellini's story, how do we know he didn't misunderstand what he's heard? There's always envy and loose talk about someone in command. That's life. My grandfather told me so."

"Clea, don't do this." Delos had an odd look on his face. "You can't ignore information like this. If there is a plot, and Biros is in it, something has to be done about it. Don't look the other way. The priest is vicious, and his position makes him even more dangerous. You're too isolated up here. You don't know what could happen."

"Do you think you know Biros better than I do?" Clea cried, stung. "I'm simply saying we don't have enough information to know what's true and what isn't. I'm not completely stupid, you know. This isn't something I can ignore. I plan to deal with this."

"I never know what to expect from you," Delos murmured, looking at Clea with what she thought might be admiration. But his next words denied it. "Of course, there's nothing you can do. This is men's work." He knelt, putting his sandals back on. "I'll look into the matter before the King is told."

"Men's work?" Clea's eyes blazed. "You and Boca are a fine pair. I doubt if there's one head between you. This is my business, not yours. Tell me what you think you can do better than I, if you can."

"Why don't you just go to the King now?" Nera put in. "What else can you do, anyway?"

"No." Delos frowned, thinking. "There are places below in the harbor where information can be found, if you know where to look. We need more proof before we sound an alarm." He started to leave, but Clea caught his arm.

She looked at him steadily. "I'm going with you."

Clea hadn't meant to say it, but once out, it seemed the practical thing to do. She was more familiar with the inner workings of the Citadel, and there was a chance she might recognize a word, a sign, before Delos could.

Delos shrugged again, a peculiar expression on

his face. "Come on, then. A few hours can't matter," he said.

"Oh, no," Nera moaned. "Clea, you know you're not supposed to leave the Citadel. It's not safe." Her voice was shrill.

Clea grabbed Nera's shoulders, shaking her to make her hear. "Father won't even know about it. We'll be back before we're missed." Nera focused on Clea's face. "I need your help, Nera," Clea told her. "Go to my room and shut the door. Stay in there until I come back. If anyone calls to you, tell them you're resting. They'll never know I'm gone."

"You mean they'll think I'm you? It won't work," Nera insisted.

"It will if you do as I say," Clea was firm. "We've got to find out what's going on. Listen, I'll give you my new necklace."

Nera pushed Clea away. "I don't want your necklace. Where would I wear it?" She turned away. "I guess I can't stop you. I'll stay in your room, but you have to tell your father it wasn't my fault when you come back. *If* you come back. . . ."

Nera's eyes filled with tears. She hugged Clea, startling her, and flew down the hall, her drape flickering in the dimming light.

Clea found Delos watching her. "What is it?" she asked. "Why are you staring at me?"

"You don't treat Nera like a servant," Delos replied. "I've seen sisters quarrel that way."

"How should I treat her?" Clea asked in surprise. "She's just Nera. I've known her for years."

"She's your slave, isn't she?" Delos persisted.

Clea waved impatiently. "Oh, no, Delos. She's

my companion. Father pays her, and I'm glad of it. You can't know how badly her family needs the money."

"A paid servant?" Delos mused. "She's no servant. She cries at the thought of danger to you. You didn't buy her friendship, you know. She gave it to you."

"I don't understand you," Clea said, puzzled. "Nera's just like that. She's . . . well, she's Nera."

"And you're Clea," Delos responded. "I see." He raced away down the hall. By the time Clea caught him, he was out of the palace and into the warm rain.

"I wish you'd stop running off like that," Clea cried. "Are you angry about something?"

"No." He was impassive. "Should I be angry?"

"I wouldn't know," Clea replied, equally brief. "But you certainly take offense easily." Delos's mouth tightened. He's as prickly as a nest of thorns, she thought.

The sentry station by the highest circle of water had been cracked by a recent earthquake. It had been pulled down, but was not yet rebuilt. The guards were nowhere to be seen. They're joking with the female kitchen slaves, Clea thought, pleased that the bridge was not guarded. She pulled a corner of her drape over her head to protect herself from the rain as she hurried over the bridge, excited. At last, she would see those fabled markets she had imagined for so long.

Clea wondered why it had never occurred to her that she could have crossed the bridge alone. At the same time she wondered if the Citadel was the safe place she'd always thought it.

Chapter 11

Clea and Delos were soon well away from the palace, approaching the second bridge and the small stone building that housed its guard. Occupied with her thoughts, Clea walked in silence. A shrine set by the path for offerings of grain and flowers caught her attention. The shrine made Clea think of Biros. She turned to look behind her, squinting to see through the rain as she walked backward.

There was no one moving about the grounds or on the west balcony of the palace. The priests will be preparing for worship soon, Clea thought, fervently hoping Biros was with them. The palace looked quite large and, with each step she took, less familiar.

"Pull your drape forward," Delos said, his voice low. He tugged at the cloth covering her hair. "We're almost there. Do you want the guards to see who you are? They'll just send you back, you know."

Quickly, Clea rearranged her drape and turned to peer at the sentry post. Two men were inside.

"Ho, Delos." The challenge was jocular. Clea ducked her head, thankful the light was poor. The rough male voice went on. "What about your old one? Has it grown tall and put on a drape?"

A thick-set guard leaned through the window. Another stood behind him, eyeing her with speculation.

"The girl up there wants him for a pet," Delos called out easily, jerking a thumb toward the palace. He gave an exaggerated shrug. "They paid well. What could I do?"

"A lot of gold? It must be, or you wouldn't have sold your brother." The man laughed loudly at his own jest.

"I made a much better bargain than you could have struck," Delos retorted, moving casually away from the building. "I'm getting wet, Nera," he added clearly, looking at Clea.

"Well, go on, then," the first guard called after them. "We can't have pretty Nera melt in the rain, eh?" He followed it with a remark made in a low tone. Both men laughed loudly.

Clea stiffened, gasping. Delos took her arm to hurry her down the path. He looked amused.

Clea twisted free to stare at Delos, her face hot. "I've never heard such a disgusting — " she began.

"No, I'm sure you haven't," Delos interrupted. "You are, after all, just Clea."

"What's that supposed to mean?" Clea cried. "How do they dare say that? If my father knew — " Clea bit back her sentence, walking carefully over the rain-slick bridge.

"I know. He'd punish them," Delos finished for her. "But you see, Nera has no father. No position, no wealth to guard against things your father protects you from. And you are Nera just now. You have to be, or you'll never get to the harbor." He glanced at her. "Are you sure you want to try this?"

"Try what?" Clea questioned.

"Are you sure you can go down the hill without giving yourself away? You're clever enough, but you won't be able to afford that royal outlook of yours. I have to agree with your father. It can't be too safe for you." He frowned. "You know, Clea, if you were recognized, you could be held for ransom. It might be wise to go back."

Go back? Give up the chance to see the markets, to be free for a few hours?

Delos shrugged as he read Clea's answer in her rebellious face. He started toward the harbor again, as if it didn't matter what she did. "Try to keep me in sight if you're coming," he tossed back.

Clea's eyes narrowed. Delos had the advantage, she saw that clearly. He knew whom to avoid, and where to fish for information. As for herself, she might be Nera to those who only knew Nera in passing, like the guards, but what about in the markets? That's where Nera lived, so who could Clea be there? Some unknown girl, tagging after a harbor boy she'd taken a fancy to? I don't like that, Clea thought with distaste, but I'm not going back now. She set her jaw stubbornly and followed Delos down the hill.

Clea caught up with Delos. "What do you think we'll find out?" she asked.

Delos stopped, looking down toward the harbor. "I've been thinking about that. Maybe our intruder was looking for something to steal, Clea. Maybe something was taken from your father's workroom." He looked grim. "If so, I will learn it below, among other things."

"But there'd be nothing to take," Clea reasoned. "Jars of herbs. Anyone could gather those. There's no point in stealing them. I still think it was Marius who ransacked Father's workroom, to get even with him. There are no valuable things in that room."

"You can't be sure," Delos said. "Remember we're Skyborn. The palace might hold ancient treasures we haven't learned of yet." He broke off and bent to scoop up a stone, straightening to fling it in the same smooth motion. "The rain's stopping," he said. "There's one more sentry post between us and the harbor. Shall we use the fog to our advantage?" He gathered a handful of stones as he spoke.

A sudden thought struck Clea. What if some of the equipment rescued by the survivors of the first down still existed? *That* could be treasure, indeed. She felt her blood pound at the prospect.

Delos suddenly pulled Clea behind a spreading shrub. "There," he whispered, crouching. He pointed through the dripping leaves. "Do you see the bridge that runs to that group of docks? And the tents beyond, can you see them?"

Clea dropped to her knees on the soggy grass. The fog had begun to billow, and it was difficult to see anything clearly. A torch shone somewhere in front of them, and voices drifted from the haloed light. Clea caught her breath and wiped the rain from her lashes. Another torch flared. She could see movement below the two fixed fires.

"They've lit the bridge. I'll draw the guards away." Delos spoke rapidly. He pulled off his sandals and slung them about his neck. "When you hear the noise, run. You'll need to get across the bridge as quickly as possible. Wait in the third tent past the first striped one to the south. I'll meet you there." With a quick intake of breath, he was gone. He was back as suddenly, surprising Clea so that she cried out in alarm. He grinned. "I forgot to tell you to carry your sandals," he whispered, and slipped into the fog again.

Clea stared after Delos, but he was already invisible. She bent to pull off her sandals. She couldn't see the bridge at all. Only a murky yellow haze showed the direction she was to take.

Clea shivered. She felt abandoned in this dim luminous world. She looked back toward the Citadel, but it had disappeared, too. The sky and the ground and everything between were white as milk. If her father knew she'd left the Citadel. . . . Clea faltered as she thought of it. But this is necessary, she told herself. This is a Skyborn's duty. A faintly guilty feeling settled in her stomach. She shifted position, anxious to be off.

A clatter of stones sounded from the north. The guards ran toward the disturbance. A command rang out and then a shout.

Clea was halfway to the bridge without remembering having started. She flew under the torches and on across the heavy stone bridge. Someone shouted hoarsely as her bare feet struck the oily wooden dock, but the tents were right there, looming up before her. She dove into a narrow path, turning north blindly.

Chapter 12

The fog lay heavily among the ragged tents. Clea
tore down the narrow, crooked footpath without
knowing where she was going. She stopped at last,
panting to catch her breath, and hugged her sandals
to her chest in relief. No one could find her in this
thick fog.

She stood between a patched and filthy tent and
a makeshift hut. The area seemed deserted. Beneath her feet the ground was hard-packed and slip-
pery, with bits of refuse kicked to both sides of the
path. Clea's toes curled up. She would have to wash
her feet before replacing her sandals.

Clea shivered, disappointed. So this was the
glamorous market Nera had led her to imagine.
Where were the shops, the fine wares, the painted
silks? Where were the gaily clad visitors to jostle,
point, and buy? This was nothing more than a
wretched garbage heap. Her nose wrinkled at an
offensive odor. Nera lied, Clea thought, morose.
She took a step forward and stopped. She couldn't
remember Delos's directions. Had he said north?
There'd been something about a striped tent. I'll
have to go back to find it, she decided.

A yelping howl filled the air, coming at Clea in a rush of sound. She stiffened. Squealing, a thin black pig burst out of the fog heading straight for her. Clea braced herself, but the pig veered and only muddied her drape. A scrawny dog flew after the pig, his nails scrabbling hard on the slick surface.

Laughing, Clea felt a tug at her hand. She whirled to see a dirty child, nearly naked and with copper hair like spiked flames, running away. Her sandals were clutched in his grimy hands.

"Stop, rat!" Clea shouted. She raced after him, dodging into the paths that separated each dingy tent from the next. "Come back, you wretched little thief!" she threatened. She almost fell, caught herself and ran on. A head came through a door-flap to stare at her, and then another, but Clea didn't care. She had to catch the boy now or else lose him in the fog. I should have done more running at the Citadel, she thought, gasping. The child's bright blue eyes looked back at Clea. He gained speed in a sudden burst, grabbed a weathered butcher's pole stuck in the ground, and threw himself around the corner.

Clea was hot on his heels. She caught the pole, but it pulled free from the ground with her weight and she flew backward. A boar's head tumbled from the sharpened end of the pole, bouncing wildly after her, scattering bits of pitch everywhere. Clea shut her eyes tightly and landed with a jarring thud. She was sprawled in mud against the side of a tent, lying half over a body. Horrified, she stared into a fleshy purple face.

"Send for the guard. Guard, guard!" The outraged voice was high and quavering. It came from a wizened old man in a bloodstained apron. He waved his bony fists angrily as he danced around Clea. She clambered to her feet, backing away. A crowd had gathered, forming a silent ring around her.

The man on the ground groaned, wheezed, and heaved himself to his knees. "I . . . I'm really sorry," Clea said, in a voice she didn't recognize as her own. A short squat woman pushed through the group to shove her face into Clea's.

"Who are you to attack my man?" the woman shouted, slapping Clea. Clea stared at her in disbelief, her ears ringing.

"Get the guard," the old man screeched, his head trembling on his thin neck. "Hold that gir-r-l. She almost killed my son. She broke my marker."

A mutter rose from the group. "What's your name?" a bearded man growled, reaching for Clea.

"Cl . . . Nera," Clea gasped, stammering. She shrank back, her cheek stinging. An arm went about her waist from behind. She fought to pull away, frantic.

"Kaneera," drawled Delos's familiar voice in her ear. His grip on Clea's waist tightened. "You were to meet me, I believe." He looked about, smiling, and the crowd stilled, watching them warily. Delos grinned and released Clea. He addressed the muck-covered man now on his feet.

"Well, Valerian," Delos said, "tell me, why are you wallowing like your pigs? I didn't know there was that much time to waste, not in this shop."

The portly man drew himself up with a glare, trying to think of a suitable insult. His jowls shook.

He does look like an angry pig, Clea thought. One of the bystanders nudged another, grinning to point at Valerian.

"She broke my sign. She'll pay for it," the old man shrilled, shaking his fist.

"I was chasing a red-haired boy," Clea cried. "He stole my sandals. I didn't mean to knock down the boar's head."

"There you are, Titus," Delos interrupted dryly, turning to the old man. "That must be Tirenus. Who else has red hair here? Speak to your son about repairing your marker, since it was your grandson who brought it about by stealing." Someone chuckled. Valerian shot a venomous look at Clea as the old man, diverted, pounced on him. The harbor folk began to drift away.

Clea's knees were weak. She could have been badly treated, and she knew it. She sighed. The old butcher had his muddy son by the arm like a child and was shaking his gnarled finger first at the boar's head and then under Valerian's nose. No one seemed to care about Clea any longer, which was just as well. Then Clea remembered her sandals and scowled.

"What about my sandals?" she said loudly.

"Be still," Delos murmured, catching her arm. The few people still watching the butcher's squabble shifted their attention back to her. "You don't learn, do you?" Delos said, looking past her shoulder.

Infuriated, Clea started to argue. Instead, she followed his intent gaze and saw a head slide cautiously around the corner of a tent. A round blue eye peered at them, blinked, and withdrew.

"There's the thief," Clea sputtered. "Did you see his red hair?"

"I need your sandals," Delos said.

"Are you mad? How can I give you what I don't have? That boy's stolen my sandals. . . ."

"Exactly," Delos told her. "That's what I meant." He disappeared before Clea could collect herself, leaving her fuming. Titus had taken his family quarrel elsewhere, and Clea was now the object of the frank attention of a cluster of ragged children. Faint sunshine slanted against the much-patched tent beside her, and she looked up into a blue sky. The fog was blowing away, and the business of the city had resumed.

Clea stepped off the path to be out of the way. She was caked with drying mud, and her hair was tangled. Somehow she had scraped her arm and it stung. Pulling her torn drape close about her neck, she nursed her damaged pride. No one would suspect me of being royal now, she thought. She tried to take comfort in it, but knew it only meant she was more vulnerable than she wanted to be. And where was Delos?

"I'm here," Delos called, as if in answer. To Clea's astonishment, the small thief bobbed at his side. The same gaunt dog she'd seen chasing the pig followed them with his tongue lolling out. She drew her drape away from the dog and frowned at the boy, who looked up at her happily.

"I'm s'posed to thank you," he lisped, with a quick grin that showed his missing front teeth. Clea shot a sharp glance at Delos who nodded toward the boy's feet.

"My sandals!" Clea cried. They were fastened about ankles far too slender for them. The child contemplated his feet with satisfaction, lifting one to admire it better. The dog watched Clea with amber eyes. "Is this what I'm being thanked for?" Clea accused. "He stole them from me so you could give them to him? Delos, you're incredible."

Nothing here was as Clea had imagined. She swallowed, blinking back tears. Why had she ever come to this wretched place, to be pushed and covered with filth and slapped. She, the granddaughter of the King.

Delos touched Clea's arm apologetically. "You have other sandals. You don't need these, Clea, and Tirenus does." She looked away, making no reply. Delos went on. "Tirenus roams the markets. He sees everything. I'm not that familiar with this section of the city. . . . He tells me Marius was here today."

Clea pushed her hair back, trying to untangle it. "Marius? The man Father — " She stopped, remembering to watch her words, but Tirenus was involved in a hopping game and was watching his feet. He wasn't listening to them, and no one else seemed to be. "Did the boy say where Marius went, or what he did?" she asked. "Is it important, do you think?"

"I don't know yet. Tirenus didn't pay any attention to Marius, but he will now. For you. He likes his sandals, you see."

Delos surveyed the crowd. "You've wasted so much time here that we'll have to depend on Tirenus to find out what we need to know about Marius. We don't want to be gone all day. I also must see a man who'll help us. Don't you know how to follow directions, Clea?"

"I? Wasted time?" Clea cried, indignant. A hooded figure jostled her in passing, and she pressed back against a tent wall. The rising babel of voices in the small clearing began to irritate her, as did the pungent odor of too many unwashed bodies.

"If you'd turned south — " Delos began.

"You said north," Clea flared, though she wasn't sure.

"Tirenus, you come here at once." Valerian's wife pushed through the crowd. She glared at Clea while jerking the child up roughly by one thin arm. Tirenus grinned over his mother's shoulder, his freckled nose wrinkling. The rangy dog gave a yawn and stretched. Someone trod on its tail, and it yelped before trotting after Tirenus.

Amused, Clea watched as Tirenus's mother angrily bore him away. Suddenly she gasped. Surely that tall man moving purposefully through the throng couldn't be Biros?

"Delos, look," Clea whispered coldly.

"I see him," Delos said. His hand circled Clea's wrist, and he melted back into the crowd, pulling her with him.

Chapter 13

"I wish the fog hadn't lifted so soon," Delos said. "I'd feel more secure about Biros not knowing we're here. What do you suppose he's doing?"

"I don't know, but I don't think he saw us," Clea said. "Can't we stop?" Delos had pulled her quickly along in a shifting route, and she was getting tired. She threw off his grip and planted her feet firmly on the path, rubbing her shoulder.

"Are you hurt?" Delos stopped to look at Clea in concern.

"I must have fallen on my arm when the pole gave way," she answered, wincing. "And you've been jerking me along like a sky-fish on a thread."

"Would you rather have your friend Biros know your business?" Delos felt Clea's shoulder. "It's not broken." He went on abruptly. "You know, Clea, you've been too sheltered. Is this your first bruise?"

Clea stiffened. "Why, yes," she drawled. "I believe it is. And, Delos, you can't know how much I appreciate the experience. You've done so much to improve my education." Delos looked at her sharply, and she returned the gaze innocently. "Oh," Clea added, inspired, "when I knocked down the boar's head? That was a well-staged lesson. Could you tell me how you arranged it?"

"You should be an actress," Delos remarked. His teeth flashed white in a smile. "You could do well at it."

"I can't imagine I'd ever need to," Clea replied. "Father is wealthy, you know." She spoke freely since no one was near enough to hear. Then she sighed. "Delos, this isn't what I expected at all," she said, making a face. "From what Nera told me, I thought the harbor would be . . . well, rich. And exciting. This is just shabby."

Delos exclaimed in exasperation. "Rich. And exciting. Clea, I hope for your sake your father keeps his wealth. Look at the sun, it's after midday. We'd better hurry."

"Where are we going? To see that mysterious friend of yours?" Clea asked, stretching her steps to keep up with Delos.

"Why are you here?" Delos asked abruptly, watching her. There was an odd note in his voice, and she looked up in surprise.

"What do you mean? You know why we're here." She shuddered at an unidentifiable maggoty heap at the side of the path.

"I hope you don't look on this trip as a pleasant outing," Delos said grimly. "If Biros . . . if Biros succeeds, your father will lose more than his wealth. I don't think you realize how serious this might be. Let's hope my friend knows more when we see him."

"I wouldn't call this a pleasant outing," Clea scoffed, but a hollow feeling began to settle in her stomach. "You started to say something, and then you changed it," she said. "Something about Biros.

What is it you're not telling me?" She caught at his arm.

Delos hesitated, glancing away. "You have too many secrets," Clea cried. "All those things Biros said about you . . . wondering if you came with a purpose, who sent you. Well, I wonder, too. And don't tell me again you were simply chasing Boca."

Delos was silent, and Clea rushed on, heedless of stares from passersby. "There's more to this than I thought," Clea said, wondering why she felt sick. "This friend of your could be my jailer, couldn't he? Is gold that important to you?"

"Clea, stop. You're not making sense." Delos pulled away, stern. "You're making a scene. People are starting to look at us."

"I don't care. I'm going home. And don't try to stop me, do you hear? Take me back to the bridge. If you don't, I promise I'll scream until someone calls a guard."

Clea's voice rose, and her last words trembled like a child's voice in the dark. Heads turned. A man in a maroon robe, thinly striped in the Egyptian manner, advanced on the two of them. His face wasn't friendly.

"Kaneera," Delos said loudly. "Please." He dropped his voice and spoke rapidly. "Clea, we're Skyborn. We must trust each other." He held her face between his hands, making her look at him. "I tell you your mother won't care," he said, lifting his voice again. "She told me so, so long as you're home by this evening."

"Is there trouble?" The suave accented voice spoke in Clea's ear. She pushed Delos away. The wearer of the striped robe, an older man, confronted her. His long green eyes were enigmatic. She stepped back, uneasy. The stranger looked amused. "I am, as you see, at your service," he said, with a short bow that set his thin earrings shivering in the sunlight.

Clea shut her eyes briefly. Skyborn, she thought with a pang. Do I really want to draw attention to us? I need to find out what Delos hasn't told me. I have to be able to trust him. She drew in a breath, resolute.

"This is a private quarrel," she told the Egyptian, noting his quick sardonic smile and braided beard. "We need no help here."

The man's gaze slid to her throat and he started, recovering himself at once. Clea's fingers went to her neck to find her gold chain. Why would he stare at that?

"Kaneera quarrels well enough without any help," Delos was saying. He looked at Clea. "Are you coming with me or not?"

The stranger's eyes were fixed now on Clea's hand. She dropped it to her side. "Yes, I'm coming," she said. The Egyptian's face was impassive as she turned away.

Clea and Delos had only gone a few steps when she felt a sound. The inner touch was so feather-light she couldn't be sure she'd heard it. *I know you*, it said, or so she thought. She shook her head to clear it. It wasn't her father. At this rate, I'll be talking out loud to myself next, she thought, mumbling like the toothless old man in our kitchens.

Clea twisted to look back at the Egyptian. He

stood in the center of the path with the crowd parting around him. His head was tilted as if he studied the sky.

Clea realized Delos was ominously quiet. Is he going to be angry? Clea wondered. "Delos, look," she said, determined that everything should be as normal as before. "See the Egyptian? He's behaving very oddly."

Delos made an impatient gesture. "Will you always suspect me?" he said, and pulled her back from the main way into a walled path. She gasped, alarmed for a moment, but they came out almost immediately to a small unexpected clearing before the docks. Boats swayed in the quiet water, their timbers gently creaking. Their masts made a leaning forest against the sky. Beneath them, a brown bear danced, circling in heavy grace to the silver-sweet tune of a pipe. A handful of bystanders, mostly ragged children, watched as the bear swung its rough head to and fro.

"We can talk here," Delos said. "No one will hear us."

"What do we have to say?" Clea asked. "We don't have time for a long talk, Delos."

Delos looked at her fiercely. "This has to be settled," he said. "You're right, we do quarrel. We fight all the time, like children, and we're not children. Why would you even think I'd try to hold you for ransom? I'm not that stupid. We can't afford not to trust each other. We pledged ourselves to the Skyborn, and you know what that means. You doubt everything about me — my actions, my motives — but I saved you from that crowd at the butcher's shop. Even before you knew me, when your father asked me to stay at the palace, you didn't want me there."

Clea flushed. It was all true, but how could she answer him when she didn't understand why herself?

Delos sighed. "I can stay down here," he said. "My rent's paid. You can find your way back to the Citadel from the bridge. We can say we never met. Will that make you happy?"

"No, Delos," Clea interrupted. "We can't go back. I guess. . . . Well, I know I was jealous of Father's interest in you, but I'm not now. He needs you. He said so." She swallowed, trying to be as honest as she knew how to be. "I'm trying to say that the reason for our being here is more important than our differences. Isn't it? We have to work together."

"You're spoiled," Delos remarked, reflecting. "And a bit ignorant."

"And you're overbearing, and equally ignorant," Clea cried. She flung her hair back to face him, eyes flashing.

"You have a vile temper."

"Oh? And you are too proud!" Clea snapped.

Delos grinned. "It seems we're evenly matched, then," he said cheerfully. "Our differences cancel out, don't they?"

Clea hesitated. "Not quite." She bit her thumbnail and then stopped, seeing the dirt that ringed it. "Delos," she said, not looking at him, "can't you see how difficult it is for me to trust you when you won't tell me what you suspect?"

"That's because I don't know," Delos replied. "Not yet. I've heard some things. That's why it's so important to ask questions in the right places, Clea."

"You didn't come to the Citadel with a message, as Biros asked? Or on any secret matters, then?" Clea persisted.

A dull red stained Delos's face. "Only my own," he muttered, surprising Clea. "Yes, I had my reasons. Perhaps if you knew, it would help."

As if Delos had finally reached a difficult decision, he plunged into speech. "All my life, I've known I was different. They don't forgive that down here. I had no parents, no home. I had my pride, you're right about that. But you can't eat pride." He scowled bitterly. Clea put out a hand to stop him, but he went on, his words savage. "They called me Prince for it. They laughed. I don't even know who named me. Can you imagine that? I was passed around from poor home to poorer home. Oh, I learned to read and write, and to speak properly. I had a friend, a cobbler, who taught me. He was very kind. He's dead now." It was as though, once started, he couldn't stop.

"Delos. . . ." Clea couldn't find the right thing to say, and he shook his head, impatient.

"Let me finish. I want to tell you. I always dreamt that one day I'd find my people. I tried to convince myself I'd been stolen as a baby. Maybe that I even belonged in a palace. . . . Anyway, when Boca ran away I was glad to find him at the Citadel. It meant I could stand, for a little while, on dirt I thought more suited to me. Another chance to pretend. Clea, I'm not sure there's any way to make you realize how I felt. I didn't belong anywhere. But your father offered me a way to change my life and I jumped at it. And then, Clea. Then. I was offered a people of my own. . . . A people that were mine, by right of birth. I am Skyborn. Do you understand what that means to me?" He stopped, his eyes blazing.

Clea was shaken. She hadn't known Delos was capable of this much emotion. Distantly, she heard the children shouting at the bear, but her whole self was concentrating on his words.

"I would die for it," Delos said. "Now do you trust me?"

Chapter 14

The ground on which they stood seemed set apart from the ordinary. The air itself quivered with his passion. Clea was deeply moved by Delos's honesty. She felt she might weep. *Ah, Delos, I do trust you. . . . Can you forgive me?* she thought, ashamed.

"Good." Relief tinged Delos's voice. He straightened, looking faintly embarrassed, and added in an offhand manner, "And, Clea, there's nothing to forgive."

Clea froze. He'd heard her. *What did you say?* she sent quickly, to make sure.

"I said, there's nothing to forgive. Listen, we've got to hurry. . . ." He stopped. "You didn't say anything," he said.

"Not aloud," Clea answered, delighted. Delos stared at her. Why did he have such a peculiar expression?

Can you hear me then? Delos questioned.

"Oh, yes," Clea replied. "Very clearly." She nodded, thinking how pleased her father would be when they told him.

"What's happening? What is this?" Delos whispered. He looked about wildly, as if he expected to find a sorcerer nearby. Why was he so disturbed? Clea put her hand on his arm and found he was trembling.

"What's wrong, Delos?" Clea asked, worried. "What are you upset about? Now we can talk whenever we want to without others knowing. That's nothing to be distressed about."

"You . . . you knew about this? You already knew how to speak this way?"

"Of course," Clea assured him, perplexed. "I could only talk with Father, though. I didn't know you could use the mind-speech. Aren't you pleased? It makes things so much easier."

Delos looked at Clea as if he couldn't see her. "Just with your father?" he asked.

Clea nodded. "Well, once, today, I saw into Nera's mind," she corrected herself. "But it's the first time anything like that ever happened. It was really an accident." She flushed, remembering the tender scene she'd stumbled into. "My father tried to contact you in the workroom when you first came to the palace," she added, "but you didn't answer, and I knew you couldn't hear him. It came to you suddenly, didn't it? Just now?"

"It's like hearing your voice. It's much smaller, but it's still your voice," Delos said, dazed. "It's really your voice."

The argument Clea had had with Biros in the palace hall flashed across her mind. She remembered that in her anger she had thrown the ancient Skyborn speech at the priest, though she had been as shocked as Biros when it happened. Could it be that strong emotion released traits Skyborn were born with? That this was the catalyst?

"Delos," Clea said, thinking as she spoke, "maybe this is how it's supposed to happen. Father said he didn't have the old speech until his sixteenth year. These gifts must come to us at different ages. Your knowing how to use mind-speech, it's like me with the ancient language. You've had the language since you were born, though you didn't understand it. Today, when I spoke in Skyborn for the first time, I knew what the words meant."

Clea shivered, seeing again the triumph in Biros's face when she had lashed out at him. She pushed the thought away. Just now it was more important that Delos stop looking at her that way, as if nothing were real. She couldn't bear it.

"Delos," Clea begged, "this is no different than seeing all those people who weren't there in the courtyard, is it?"

"You don't know what's happened," Delos said. "I know now what it was. I've heard this before."

"What do you mean?" Clea asked.

"I shut it out," Delos went on, his speech ragged. "When the voice came to me, when I was a child. I used to hide, put my hands over my ears." His face held despair.

"You've been reached before?" Clea asked sharply.

"Yes. It was a man's voice, echoing in my head. . . . It was my father, I know that now. I thought I was mad, or possessed. Maybe even that it was a voice from the dead. I was afraid."

Clea stared at him. "Are you sure it was your father?"

Delos bowed his head. She could hardly hear him. "He said so, and I wouldn't listen, you see. All those times he tried. He begged me to speak to him, to help him find me. There'd been a shipwreck, he said. And he cried, once. He cried, Clea. Now, I find it was true. It was my father's voice, and I wouldn't listen."

"Are you saying your father is alive somewhere, and doesn't know where you are?" Clea could hardly take it in.

Delos raised miserable eyes to hers, his lashes wet. "It's been a long time since I heard it. He must be dead."

"You'd give up because of that?" Clea cried. She remembered herself and looked to see if anyone listened. The crowd watching the dancing bear had grown, but no one watched Clea and Delos. The piper played in a minor key, and the lilt of the tune had changed. It was a haunting sound. The sunlight slanted, throwing afternoon shadows. Clea thought of Ranson, with his world lost, and felt a sudden urgency. Hurry, we must hurry, she thought.

"Delos, we'll find your father," Clea said uneasily. "Surely he's still alive. But with no answer from you, he'll be looking somewhere else for you. Father can help us. Shouldn't we go?"

Clea, where are you? The message was thrown at her, strong and insistent. Clea caught her breath.

"It's Father," she said flatly. "Now I'm really in trouble. He knows I've left the Citadel. Could you hear him?" Delos shook his head and lifted a hand. He wore a look of expectancy.

"Something . . ." Delos muttered. His head tilted, listening.

Clea, answer me. Her father again. Clea cast a despairing look at Delos and replied.

I'm here, she sent. *I'm by the Seaway, with Delos.*

Come home. Now. There was a flurry, a dimming of contact, and then the message came through strongly again. *There's grave danger. Bring Delos with you. There's no time to explain. Hurry, daughter.*

Clea's stomach knotted. Biros must have made his move while she and Delos were away from the palace. *That's why we came here*, she sent quickly. *We came to find information about Biros's plot. I know you're angry*, she added, flinching against the answer she expected.

Biros? came Taland's sharp reply. *We know of that. Biros is a minor matter now. Come home at once.*

A minor matter? What could be worse than the loss of the throne? White, she reached for Delos's arm. He looked down at her, his gaze clearing. Had he been listening, too?

Something tugged at Clea's drape. She jerked away violently and then saw it was the boy, Tirenus. The copper tumble of his hair blazed in the low-angled sunlight.

"Tirenus," Delos's voice was vibrant. Clea thought he looked different, older perhaps. His arm rippled beneath her fingers. It made her think of the time she had stood before a caged panther, controlled and sleek and dangerous. Delos is like that, Clea thought, letting her hand drop away.

"That Marius." The child grinned and wiped his grubby hand across his nose, leaving a pale streak. "He came down today to sell, but nobody bought."

"Something he'd stolen?" Delos asked. The child nodded.

"That's right. Old Fisheye split his sides laughing. Trash, he said it was. Fisheye wouldn't give him a broken coin for it. . . ."

"Where'd he get it? What was it?" Clea broke in, wanting to hurry him.

"Works at the palace, don't he?" The boy's tone was derisive. "Marius stole it up there, didn't he? Where else? There's nothing down here to take."

"What was it, Tirenus?" Delos asked. The child looked at him with the respect he'd refused Clea, and it angered her.

"Fisheye told my father it was a little piece of heavy stuff," Tirenus replied. "Not even honest metal. Marius said it was a sorcerer's stone."

Clea stared at Delos. Marius had come back to the palace to steal. Had he been the intruder in the hall the day she and Delos were told about the Skyborn?

Tirenus was still talking. "Old Fisheye," he snickered, his bony shoulders twitching, "he told Marius to make a bag of coins with it, instead of trying to sell it. That's when Marius shouted at him." The boy laughed.

"I wish I'd seen it," Delos said fervently. Tirenus beamed.

"Oh, Delos, what does this matter now?" Clea cried. "We've got to go home. Come on. Didn't you hear Father?"

"No. I was otherwise occupied." Delos pushed the boy's shoulder gently. "The bear's still dancing. Don't you want to watch it?"

"I'm not interested in that stupid bear," Clea said, her voice shaking. Tirenus hopped away into the crowd surrounding the piper.

"We must hurry," Delos said.

"Father — " Clea began.

"We're not going to the palace. If Marius couldn't sell the piece to Fisheye, he'd try Simon. That's where we're going." He was already moving, dodging into a winding path away from the water. The sunlight was peculiarly metallic.

"Wait, wait," Clea cried, running after Delos. Out of breath, she caught him. "It doesn't matter anymore if Marius stole something from the palace," she said. "And Father said Biros doesn't matter. He said to come now, that there's grave danger." Clea grew cold as she remembered her father's warning.

"Didn't you hear Tirenus?" Delos threw over his shoulder. "He said Marius called it a sorcerer's stone. It must be a Skyborn tool. We have to find it. It won't take long."

"But, Father said — "

Delos interrupted tersely. "My friend Simon is a jewelsmith. I rent a bed there. I know Marius — he'd sell the piece to be melted down for metal if he had to, and he'd have to take it to Simon. I must go there." They were back on the main path, weaving their way through crowds of shoppers. A bold-eyed girl with brilliant cheeks hailed Delos, and he nodded his head in greeting. The girl stared at Clea. Annoyed, Clea felt her face redden.

"Biros was down here to find that piece. I know it. He mustn't have it," Delos said. "He certainly wasn't looking for us."

"How do you know?" Clea asked.

Delos shrugged. "We're not important enough for his personal attention," he said. "He'd have sent someone else after us instead."

Clea's voice was hoarse. "Delos, you've got to listen to me," she insisted, stepping around a beggar. She stumbled, and Delos caught her elbow and pushed her around a corner, his fingers across her lips. Moments later, Clea watched Biros stride past, his massive shoulders hunched in anger.

"He didn't find it," Delos said with grim satisfaction. "I told you it was important." He pulled Clea back into the crowd, turned beneath a stone arch, and ducked into a low doorway.

A gaunt face, which seemed lit from within by fire, rose. It seemed to float in the dark room, and Clea made a tiny strangled sound as it moved toward them.

Chapter 15

"You need your lamps, the sun's behind the clouds," Delos said, moving easily into the room. "Do you want me to light them for you, Simon?"

"Ah, please. Thank you, Delos," the face sighed, sinking again. Fascinated, Clea watched the man himself begin to appear in the gloom. Delos lit straw from the minuscule forge over which the jewelsmith sat to light the lamp wicks. Then he brought a lamp to Simon's table, against which leaned a cripple's stick. It was a comfortable room, though crude. There were stools, two couches, and miniature tools strewn on the table.

"I've missed you, Delos," Simon remarked, with a quick sidelong stare at Clea. He covered the forge as he spoke.

"I'm glad to see you, too," Delos said, pulling a stool around for Clea and one for himself. "This is a friend of mine, and closer than a friend," Delos explained as he seated himself. He motioned for Clea to do the same. "Her name is Clea," Delos went on.

Clea couldn't believe it. Why would Delos tell this man who she was, after all the trouble they'd taken to hide her identity? We really have no time for this, she thought, worrying.

The smith's bushy white eyebrows lifted. "There is a motherless girl named Clea in the King's household," he said. He shrugged. "That's not important, of course. Closer than a friend, you say? Well." He pointed to a small cupboard against the wall. "I'd be honored if you'd accept something to drink, Clea. Delos?"

"I don't think there's time. . . ." Clea began, but Delos was already pouring. She accepted the cup with a murmur, sat, and lifted it to her lips. She wasn't prepared for the biting flame of the first swallow. Her eyes watered, and she set the cup down hastily. Delos had set his cup aside without tasting it.

"The one thing I feel no need to forgive the gods for is this," the old man nodded. He drank again, savoring the taste Clea found so bitter.

"I've heard things in the markets, Simon," Delos began. "Disturbing things."

"So?" Simon reached for the slender jug, pouring another cup. He shot a glance at Delos. "Sometimes it's better not to hear too much."

"You've told me there's a time for hearing, a time for all things," Delos said. His eyes, wide and shining, were fixed on Simon's face. "There's a time for knowing who a friend may be, for helping that friend."

"Or one who's closer than a friend? I see. Tell me, have you finally found out who you are, then?" Simon asked.

Delos hesitated only for a moment. "Yes," he answered firmly. "Yes, I have." He waited, but Simon only stared into his cup, turning it slowly. He seemed lost in thought.

Delos, please, Clea threw at him. *We can't stay here. We need to be doing, not talking.*

Wait, Delos sent, watching Simon's craggy face.

The floor quivered, settled, then shook again more strongly. Clea looked up, alert, but the tremor slowed and stopped. The two at the table were intent on each other. Clea knew they had to leave. Her flesh prickled. *It's really too hot, much too hot,* she thought, shifting on her seat.

Please, Delos, she sent again impatiently, but he ignored her.

"Do you think Biros would be a better king than Larok, Simon?" Delos persisted calmly.

"I've heard things, too." The smith stared at Delos. "Treachery from within, and Biros rewarded with a crown? It's just possible — "

"No!" Clea cried. Why had her father told her Biros was nothing to be concerned about?

"Kingdoms come and go," Simon was saying. He reached a long brown finger to the table and drew a circle in the moisture left by the jug. "That's the way of things. Larok or another king, it matters little to me. I make my wares and sell them, and find happiness where I can." Lifting his head, he held Clea with a bitter gaze.

"Simon," Delos said softly, "can you support a traitor by your silence?"

"I'd rather leave war to kings, but . . . No. I can't." The smith smiled faintly. "I'm tired, Delos, not evil. For what it's worth, you may have all I know. Tell King Larok that Biros is organizing a rebellion. He has both supplies and soldiers. The

King can make of it what he will." He shrugged and drained his cup, putting it down with a little thump.

"The King will thank you," Delos told him, rising.

"I doubt it," Simon remarked wryly. "Bad tidings, like spoiled squid, are never welcome."

There was a distant rumble like thunder, and Clea saw the lamps flare. Shadows moved across the rough stone walls as the flames dipped. Like fleeing swallows, Clea thought, or the caged bird she had freed as a child. But it's not the season for big storms, she thought, so angry at what she'd heard that her mind darted about. She'd only been caught out of the palace once in a storm, and her father had found her and brought her home. *Home.* The word steadied her.

"We must leave," Clea insisted. "Come, Delos."

"Your father will be concerned about you," Simon said. Clea looked at him sharply. "I made your gold chain, girl," he told her. "I don't forget my work. I suppose Delos is working at the Citadel? Yes. Well, I can't imagine the King knows you're away from the palace with him, but he's steady. You'll come to no harm. I will say, though, if you want to go undetected, you might wear clothing of coarser material. Even the mud on it won't disguise its quality." He pushed the cover of his forge aside.

Delos and Clea stared at each other. "I hadn't thought of that," Delos said, his face blank.

"So I see," the smith remarked. He reached for his small leather bellows, surveying the embers with a critical eye.

The sorcerer's stone, Clea remembered. *Delos, ask him.*

I hadn't forgotten, Delos sent with a frown. He

turned back at the door. "Oh, Simon," he said, as if in an afterthought. "You might keep watch for a bit of metal taken from the palace."

Simon snorted. "I've already seen it, if you mean that amulet Marius tried to peddle to me. I wouldn't waste time looking at it. It can't be valuable, and the metal is far too hard to beat into anything else." He plied the bellows vigorously, puffing new flame into the charred wood.

"You didn't buy it, then?" Delos asked, disappointed.

The old man shook his head. "I try to stay away from stolen work, you know that. I might have been interested if there really were such things as sorcerer's stones. But who believes that in this age?"

"Then Marius still has it," Clea said. "Come on, Delos, let's go."

"No, he doesn't," the smith said. "The Egyptian took it."

"Egyptian?" Delos questioned. "When?"

"You seem quite concerned," Simon commented. "Marius has taken things from the palace before. Why is this piece so important?" He squinted at Delos.

Delos exhaled. "Look, Simon," he said, "I don't know what it is, but it belongs to Clea's father. Marius has been dismissed from the Citadel, and I've taken his place, so I know." The smith's lips pursed in surprise, and Delos nodded. "If I could get it back — "

"Taland would be sure he made a wise choice in replacing Marius with you," Simon concluded. "Ah, Delos. Haven't I always said you'd go far?" He laughed.

"Never mind that," Delos said. "Did you know this Egyptian?"

The smith waved his pincer. "Who knows any of these foreign buyers? There are too many of them these days. He didn't give his name, and I didn't ask for it. I'd just told Marius 'no' for the third time when a hand came down on the amulet. I looked up, and there stood the Egyptian, with those eyes of his staring fire at me, like . . ." He broke off, shaking his head. "He said something in a language I'm not familiar with, said he'd take it, paid Marius, and left."

"Eyes," Clea repeated. "Braided beard? Maroon robe, striped?"

"You've seen him? Very nice, those earrings he wore. Not Egyptian, though." He frowned, trying to place the workmanship. "They were old. Quite thin and old. Two hundred years at least, I should think."

Clea bit her lip. There was no time to search for the Egyptian, and he wouldn't part with his prize, anyway. It was disturbing to think that one of the ancient tools — if that's what it was — should be sold as jewelry, but it had happened.

"Well," Delos said. "At least friend Biros didn't get it."

Simon held his thumb and forefinger apart, the length of an egg. "He missed buying it by only that much," he told them. "The Egyptian had left moments before." A grim smile crept across his face. "I might add that he was most unhappy."

"Did Biros dare threaten you?" Delos cried, his eyes burning.

"Wouldn't you expect him to? And so, of course,

I threw him out," the old man chuckled, gleeful.

"But how . . . ?" Clea began. She stopped suddenly. The smith was crippled, but she didn't need to point it out.

Simon's grin was broad. "I flung a burning ember at his arrogant belly with my pincer," he said. "Biros hopped away quickly, I can tell you. And when I mentioned the next one would be aimed at his nose, he took his leave. Bellowing like a bull," the old man added with relish. "Rhanjhon himself couldn't have let out such a roar."

Sudden laughter rocked the room. "I'd like to have seen him," Delos gasped.

"Oh, you will," Simon cried, wiping his streaming eyes. "You will. He hates you, you know. He accused me of giving the piece to you." He beat his hand against his knee, and choked with mirth, exploded, "He thinks you've got it. A fine joke, eh?"

Chapter 16

Clea straightened outside the low door of Simon's shop. The air was touched with an uncanny light. Although the sun had already dipped in the west, its rays, still strong, threw light against the inverted brass bowl that was the sky. The shimmering horizon was smeared with purple shot through with flickering crimson. Clea shivered. It was hot, too . . . an odd, airless heat that left her lips parched. She ran her tongue across them — they were as sulty as the sea — and stood watching the sky.

"It looks as if a storm is rising," Delos said.

"It isn't the season for the big storms, Delos, you know that. And that isn't a storm cloud."

Delos shrugged. "Storms have been known to come out of season. The sky does look ominous, though," he added. He jerked his head toward the path. "We're finished here. We'd better start back to the palace. Your father will begin to worry."

Clea agreed. There was nothing she wanted more than to reach the palace. Once on the main path, she felt relieved that they were on the way. Still, something seemed wrong. The area was nearly deserted. An old man pushed by them, running, and far ahead a woman with a heavy bundle disappeared around a corner in frantic haste.

"Where is everyone?" Clea asked, surprised.

Delos shook his head. "It's usually more busy at this time of day," he said. "Clea, did your father mention what he's concerned about?"

"No," she replied, but apprehension weighted her chest. As they hurried north toward the harbor bridge, she saw buildings closed tight, with barred windows. And where were the children?

The skin over Delos's cheekbones was taut, as if he were filled with tension. Clea remembered he'd been like that at the docks, where the bear danced. She frowned.

"You told me you hadn't heard Father's message, back there," she said. "Why?"

"I was listening to another voice."

"Another voice?" Clea cried, startled. "Delos, was . . . could it have been your father?"

"I . . . don't really know. It was all very strange. I've been thinking about it." Delos glanced over his shoulder and began to walk a little faster. "Something feels wrong, Clea. It's more quiet here than I've ever seen it."

Clea hardly heard that. Only the fact that a message had been sent by an unknown person concerned her right now. "What did the voice say? Was it a man?" she persisted.

"Yes, a man's voice. It was distant, though. I couldn't hear it as clearly as I heard yours. *Are you there?* he asked, and I answered. Then he asked my name, my city of birth, and of course . . ." Delos's voice trailed off and he shrugged.

"Go on," Clea urged, stopping in the path to peer

at him. The sunlight was dim, almost dusky, though it was still afternoon.

"That's all. Except he told me we'd meet, and I said I had a lot to do. Then he said, *Later will do as well. Take care of the girl.* He seemed amused."

"Take care of the girl," Clea repeated. "Are you sure it wasn't the King? I've never used the mind-speech with him, but he must know it."

Delos shook his head irritably. "I know the King's voice. Why would he say something like that? It wasn't the King."

"Then who? Another Skyborn, of course. I'd at least have asked his name," Clea said.

"Do you think I'm a fool?" Delos shot back. "I did ask. He said it mattered little who he was, but rather what he was."

"We really don't have time to talk about it," Clea said uneasily. A sense of urgency broke over her like a cold wave, and she caught her breath. "Please, Delos, let's hurry," she begged.

"You're right," Delos said, shaking himself. He set off again quickly, with Clea beside him.

"Ho. Stop there." A challenge rang out. Clea whirled to see a pair of men approaching. Their wrapped ankles identified them as harbor guards. One pointed his sword. "Stand, thief," he shouted.

"What is this?" Clea gasped.

"It's Biros's doing. It must be," Delos muttered. "I'll slow them down. Get to the palace. Tell the King. Go, Clea." He shoved her away, crouching to meet the guards as they ran toward him. Clea flew blindly in the direction he'd pushed her. The sound of a grunting struggle beat at her ears. Then there was a muffled cry, cut short.

Clea flung a frantic look over her shoulder and saw Delos on the ground with a guard bent over him. The other guard was gaining on her. His naked sword flickered as he ran. He mustn't catch me, she thought desperately. At that moment the path heaved, tossing her carelessly against the stones. A thin note rang in her head. She slid down to the ground with both hands pressed hard on the packed dirt. The earth reared again, groaning, and the wall of the house opposite Clea cracked slowly. A gap slithered open from bottom to top before her dazed eyes.

The guard hauled her roughly to her feet. The ground rumbled, a long continuous sound. Clea was taken back to where she'd started. Delos stood shaking his head to clear it. His wrists were tied, and there was a darkening bruise across his cheek. Clea was filled with sudden anger.

"Release him," she ordered, twisting out of her captor's grasp. Laughing, the guard caught her wrists and bound them with a short cord. Clea stared at her hands and stepped back. Her dark eyes blazed. "My father will have you flogged," she shouted.

Delos threw a warning look. *Careful*, he sent. *There are two of them, and their swords are sharp.*

"Ho, a spitting cat," the bearded guard rasped. He grinned. "Who is your father, cat, that is, if you even know that?"

Clea gasped at the insult. "I'm granddaughter to King Larok, you poor fool," she cried. "Free us, now."

"And me? I'm the favorite son of Rhanjhon," the taller man said, with a mincing note in his voice.

"Come now, girl, you can do better than that." His bored eyes ran over her filthy drape, and he jerked his chin in the direction of the Citadel. "Everyone knows of the great baths up there, and you haven't seen water for some time. Besides, we answer to Biros now, not the former King."

"Here, what's this?" the other asked, his gaze on Clea's throat. He pulled Clea's chain over her head, catching it in her long hair. She cried out as he yanked it free. Delos leaped forward, his face flushed with anger, but the tall guard knocked him back against the wall.

"Gold." The bearded man held up the finely worked chain. His eyes were greedy. "Handsome work. Is this what the boy took from the temple?"

"No," Delos interrupted hoarsely. "It's hers. Give it back to her." The guard laughed again.

"Well, Biros can have you, and welcome," he said. "But it's only right we should have a little something for our trouble, eh?" He tucked the chain away, grinning. "Don't worry, girl. It should be a simple matter for you to steal another. If you're able, that is, when the priests are through with the pair of you."

"Biros wanted the boy," the tall guard protested languidly. "He said nothing about this girl."

Father. I need you. Clea threw all her angry strength into the call, but met only a swimming void that she couldn't bridge. He'd never failed to answer before. She tried again. *Father.* There was still no response. Delos, she saw, stared straight ahead. A muscle at the angle of his jaw twitched.

I can't reach Father, Clea sent. Delos turned his head to look at her.

Wait, he replied. His eyes were shadowed. A low murmur from somewhere came, rising and falling, but it wasn't the sea. The sound was too uneven. It was like nothing Clea had ever heard. Bees? Was it the sound of hiving? Not in a city, surely.

"Ah. Fine work. Biros will be pleased you've caught the thief." The faintly accented voice came from behind Clea. She twisted to see. A cowled priest moved serenely toward them, his lower face hidden by a fold of blue. Long eyes, with fine wrinkles at the corners, considered Delos and Clea. "I'll take them with me," he said with satisfaction.

Clea knew Bellini was the only new priest. Then who could this be? Delos looked impassive, but Clea saw relief in his posture. She thought quickly. Between them, she and Delos might be able to escape from one man more easily than two. And if this stranger were really a priest, he'd be slack from soft living. She ducked her head to hide the hope she felt.

"Take them? You?" asked one of the guards. "If you please, honored priest," he said, too politely, "Biros gave no orders about the girl." He let his voice die away.

"Oh?" The priest's brows lifted in surprise. "Obviously an oversight. He distinctly spoke to me about her. He seemed quite anxious, in fact, to obtain Kaneera as well as this Delos." Shocked at the use of her false name, Clea looked up to meet amusement in the stranger's eyes. "You are known, Kaneera. Indeed, I know you," he said.

Confused, Clea frowned, trying to remember where she had heard those words before. The priest turned to the guards. "I'm sure Biros will want to reward your efforts. We'll need to use you again, perhaps," he said, dismissing them with a graceful gesture.

"We'll walk with you," the bearded man said smoothly, his hand resting on his sword hilt. "To be sure of Biros's thanks, and to assist you," he added with a grin. To be sure of Biros's gold, Clea thought contemptuously.

"I need no assistance. I have . . . powers," the priest replied. His voice was cold. "You'd be better served to return to your work, I think. Listen." He tilted his head, watching the guards. In the silence, Clea heard the garbled murmur which had caught her attention earlier. It had grown in intensity and held the chilling sound of fear.

"What is it?" the taller guard cried.

"It's a sudden madness that comes upon men," the priest replied. His voice deepened, and his eyes gleamed in the ruddy light. "The city is in flight. Go and see for yourselves. When earth speaks and the sky fills with blood. . . ."

Clea stared at the priest as the guards, backing away from his luminous gaze, broke and ran toward the Seaway.

Chapter 17

The running footsteps of the guards died away quickly, lost in the rising clamor from the Seaway. The path was filled with an eerie light. Even the shadows were tinged with it, as if thin ochre had spread over the walls and the hard dirt path. It would look like this if the sun were dying, Clea thought, feeling sick. She saw Delos shudder.

"Who are you?" Delos's voice was curiously young. The blue-robed stranger smiled, his eyes crinkling as he spoke.

"I believe I've mentioned that who a man is may not be as important as — "

"As what he is?" Delos interrupted. "It was you, then? The voice I heard, before. And you heard my call for help this time. . . ." He stopped. He was pale, his bruised cheek dark. "You're not my father, are you?"

The man shook his head. "No. But if I'm right, he was my friend." He looked at Delos with compassion. A message passed between them, and Delos closed his eyes as if struck by a blow.

So his father is dead, Clea thought, sorrowful. She stared at the priest and found her voice. "You're the Egyptian," she accused. "You're no priest."

"How very true," he replied calmly. "And how very fortunate for you that I am." He pushed back the cloth from his face and produced a short flashing knife. His beard was gone. If it hadn't been for his eyes, Clea wouldn't have known him.

The Egyptian cut Clea's bonds neatly and turned to free Delos while she rubbed her reddened wrists. "We don't have much time," the man told them. "The Seaway is so crowded that a ship can barely get through it to open water. Do you hear that sound? It's the sound of fear. People are fleeing Atlantis." He shook his head gravely.

"But why?" Clea shot back. "There have always been times when the earth shakes. Why are they afraid of it now?"

The Egyptian shoved his knife into his wide girdle. "It isn't just that. The city is in panic. It's believed that Rhanjhon has abandoned his island . . . that everyone will die, if not by the earthshaker, then on the points of the rebel's swords. And of course. . . ." He paused, rubbing his chin as if looking for the beard that once hid it.

"Yes?" Delos prompted.

The man frowned, glanced at Clea, and then said abruptly, "They blame the King for Rhanjhon's displeasure. Biros did his work well. Whispers of evil have been fanned to a flame, and you, my girl, are far from safe here."

Clea stared at him. "How do we know we can trust you?" Her voice was clear. "You seem to know us, but where did you get your robe? You could still be Biros's man."

"Has danger dulled your wits?" the Egyptian demanded. "Do the priests know the mind-speech? Look." He thrust out his hand — the star was there, in his palm. "I must go to the Citadel at once. Come or stay, as you wish. As for the robe," he said cheerfully, "I traded my false beard for it, to a red-haired child outside the public baths. I thought I might need it. As you see, it has served well." He spread his hands wide. Tirenus, Clea thought wryly. Is nothing sacred to him?

The Egyptian turned away, and a chuckle floated in the air. "There's a naked priest in the city today who no doubt wishes to find me," he said, and walked quickly in the direction of the harbor bridge.

Clea shivered, wishing they had gone to the King at once, as Nera had begged her to. They'd only wasted precious time below the hill, and now they were all in danger. Nera had done her best to warn them, but Clea hadn't listened. It still seemed unreal to her, as if this were a bad dream from which she would wake.

"It's not a dream," Delos said. "We simply didn't know Biros had already set his plot in motion."

"I'm sorry about your father," Clea ventured awkwardly.

Delos looked stricken. "I let myself hope he was alive. Now, at least, I have the Skyborn. We must get to the palace, Clea."

They began to run and caught up to the Egyptian at the harbor bridge. He stood watching the sentry post across the water. There was an air of abandonment about it.

"We travel together," the Egyptian remarked.

"Good. I haven't given my name. It's Senkhet." He inclined his head gravely.

"And mine is not Kaneera, but Clea," she told him. He nodded, his earrings glimmering in the dusky air.

"I see you don't remember me from the gathering when you decided to accept the destiny of the Skyborn," he said. "I stood by your mother." At Clea's look of surprise, the Egyptian nodded again, reflecting. "I didn't have as far to come as your mother. I was on a ship bound for here at the time. It seems long ago, doesn't it?" They were across the wide bridge now, on the path that led to the Citadel.

Clea looked up at the palace, high against the lurid sky. It, too, seemed deserted. "You didn't know me at first, there in the marketplace," she told the Egyptian.

"My dear girl. You were wearing so much mud," Senkhet protested, amused. "Had you been frolicking with pigs?"

Delos gave a short mirthless laugh. "You're close to the mark," he said, watching the terrain.

Clea peered at the temples ahead, alert for any movement, but she saw nothing. Still, something nagged at her — something she'd overlooked. What can it be? she thought uncomfortably. Then she turned to look back, and her breath left her in a gasp.

"Delos," she exclaimed, pointing. "The great harbor is empty." The ships and barges were gone, and the water was motionless. A desolate feeling crept into Clea's chest.

"Yes." Senkhet stood beside her. "Rats leave a doomed ship, but men must take the ship with them. Didn't you notice it when we crossed the bridge?" Clea shook her head.

"They've all gone to the Seaway to try to get through it to open water," Delos said. "If it's as full of ships as you say, they'll never get out." Clea hadn't realized how much she'd counted on a ship for escape until Delos said it, and it frightened her.

"This is quite dangerous. A difficult situation." Senkhet fell silent, and Clea felt the ground tilt beneath her feet. This can't be happening, she told herself. Still, the harbor is empty. I can see it, so that must be real. She stared at the Egyptian, trying to catch the thoughts that whirled in her mind like blown leaves. Why hadn't she been able to reach her father? Perhaps the Egyptian knew.

Senkhet looked at Clea. The lines about his mouth were deep. "You must be brave," he said. "I can't reach either the King or your father, though I communicated with both of them earlier."

"What do you mean?" Clea cried. "What need is there for courage?" Delos moved to touch Clea's shoulder, and she looked up, startled.

Senkhet frowned. "Clea, listen to me. If I can't reach them, it means only two things. Either they are in the deepest sleep . . . that is, unconscious . . . or they have gone beyond that, to death."

"They aren't dead," Clea said politely. "I would know it." She saw Senkhet's doubt. "I would," she shouted. She pushed Delos's hand away. What good was it to be Skyborn if it meant losing her father? He isn't dead, she thought. I'll never believe it. The

Egyptian is stupid, and cruel, and I'll tell my father
to send him away. I'll tell him to put Biros in chains,
too.

"There's something odd here," Delos said slowly.
"Listen."

"What should I hear?" Clea asked, hating the
quiver in her voice. She wiped her eyes with the
back of one hand, the only clean spot she could find.
Senkhet's head was tipped, listening. Clea heard
nothing but the voiceless murmur from the Seaway,
and she had become accustomed to that.

"The swallows. And the sea birds. Where are
they?" Delos asked, puzzled.

"Oh, not the swallows," Clea cried, shaken.
"Have they gone, too?" She felt something close to
despair.

"There is more here than I was sent for. More
than I expected to find," Senkhet murmured. His
face was brooding, his eyes intent as he searched
the sky. Clouds moved swiftly across the sullen bril-
liance that spread up from the horizon.

"Why were you sent for, then? Why did you
come, and in a false beard?" Clea demanded.

"You must know Skyborn are beardless. The
beard was a disguise, a small precaution," the Egyptian replied absently. "You see, we knew about Biros's scheme, but the panic in the city is out of
proportion. My talent, feeble though it is, lies in
the art of rule." Senkhet lifted his shoulders in a
self-deprecating shrug, and his perplexed gaze held
Clea's. "I came to consult with Larok, to advise
about Biros. Until I reached the island and walked
the city, I saw no need for great concern. Now. . . ."
He gnawed his lip.

"What is it then? What's wrong?" Delos asked, shifting uneasily.

"I'm filled with mystery," Senkhet said. "I know nothing, but I sense that something vast and terrible moves across the sky. Your father keeps our star charts," he told Clea. "Has he said anything to you about this?"

"No. I know so little about the charts," Clea replied. "He did say not to worry about the earth-shaker."

"The time for disaster is not yet here," Delos broke in. "I, myself, heard Taland say that." He scowled. "I don't believe Clea's father is dead, nor the King. I don't understand any of this."

Senkhet shook his head in annoyance. "Nor do I. Still, the birds have gone. That seems to be an ill omen. Clea, is there a way into the palace that would be secret? Unguarded? I'd like us to remain unseen until we know more."

"There's an east door that's seldom used," Clea offered.

Impatiently, Delos spoke. "Why search for a secret way into the palace?" He flung an arm wide, taking in the slope. "If Biros holds the Citadel, we've already been seen."

Without a word, Senkhet resumed his steady pace up the hill. "My dear Delos," he said, as if speaking to a child, "the sentry posts seem abandoned. I see no one on the grounds, so there is a chance that we haven't been detected. Shouldn't we use that chance?" Delos frowned, and the Egyptian went on. "This path has the only bridges, as you know. Do you know any other way to approach the Citadel?"

Delos flushed, and Clea looked away to spare him. This Egyptian is a most uncomfortable man, she thought.

They crossed the middle bridge without challenge. The ground continued to shift and she put her feet more firmly on the path. The hollow rumble died away, leaving the air quivering. What could drive the birds away? Clea thought. They'd know nothing of Biros. Then she remembered her father's message. Grave danger, he'd said. Grave, indeed, if even the birds fled. . . .

They walked in silence, each preoccupied, until at last the palace loomed before them, just beyond the final bridge. The Egyptian stopped, eyeing the grounds past the fallen sentry post. Clea wondered what lay within the familiar white walls of the palace. The grass was still, the leaves on the nearby trees motionless.

Senkhet turned to Clea with a bow. "So. The east door. Will you show me?"

Clea crossed the bridge, her gaze fixed on her home. First she would find her father, and then — But as she took her first step off the bridge, someone seized her. There was a swirling confusion, a sudden fierce scuffle made more frightening by the silence of the attackers. She flung her head back to stare at the man who held her, and her spirits sank. The priests had been behind the broken stones, waiting. They had escaped the harbor guards only to fall into the hands of Biros's men.

Chapter 18

The three of them were bound in silence and jostled roughly along the path. Though it was only late afternoon, the brilliant horizon had dimmed to the purple of an early dusk. Clea looked at Delos in despair.

We're not dead yet, Delos sent. He tripped on a rock the earthshaker had lifted from its bed, and caught himself.

The Egyptian's enigmatic eyes were serene. Blood welled slowly from a cut in his lip, staining his chin. *At least we will be at the center of the plot,* he sent. How can he be so calm? Clea thought angrily. He has to realize the danger, but he seems amused. This is no game. Senkhet's brows moved slightly. *Clea, do you believe Biros can outwit Skyborn?*

Senkhet. Senkhet. Is it you? The words came faintly and ended in a throb of pain that made Clea wince. Could that be Grandfather? She caught her breath in a gasp. The priest holding her arm gave her an odd look and moved a little away.

Are you safe, my friend? And Taland? Senkhet's question was intense, almost a shout.

I am . . . alive. Taland is not with me. My head. . . . The voice trailed off, groaning. Clea realized he'd been struck unconscious. The King's alive, and surely Father is, too, Clea thought. She shut her eyes in relief and immediately pitched forward with a cry, striking her chin as she fell. She sprawled on the steps of the palace entrance with her bound hands beneath her.

A bulky priest Clea only knew slightly pulled her to her foot. Without a word, he shoved her into the entry after Delos and Senkhet. Only a few lamps smoked in the walls. So the servants have fled, Clea thought. She counted their captors. Seven men held them, out of the thirty that served Rhanjhon. That left twenty-three priests — no, twenty-one — unaccounted for. One was stuck in the public baths, she remembered, and Biros would make the thirtieth. Would Nera's friend Bellini try to help them against so many?

When they entered into the long, pillared hall, a drift of sound came to meet them. It was a soothing ripple of strings. Clea recognized the instrument's voice. Her father had made it himself from the best mountain woods and was teaching her to play. She shook with rage. How dare anyone touch her chorder? How *dare* Biros harm the King? She was swept into the throne room on a wave of anger unlike any she'd ever known, only to be placed like a chess piece before the throne.

Clea's chorder was placed negligently across a blue-robed lap. A square hand plucked four crisp descending notes with a strange delicacy, then swept into a brutal discordant crash. It rang through the room, jarring and painful, and Clea's head snapped up. Biros smiled at her pleasantly, caressing the chorder to a ghost of a tune. He wore her grandfather's silver band about his oiled hair.

I will kill him, she thought coldly.

Watch your tongue, sent the Egyptian. *You can't help your Father if you're dead.*

"We are pleased to see you, Clea," Biros said, still smiling. "So, you've run off with the harbor rat, leaving Nera in your place. Did you enjoy your outing? How clever you must feel." Clea said nothing. Had he harmed Nera? She could not show that it mattered. She wouldn't give Biros that weapon. "Of course," the priest mused, "we didn't discover Nera until after we had arranged a suitable end for the previous King. . . ." He paused, watching Clea greedily.

Clea kept her face still, her eyes expressionless, thankful she already knew the King was alive. She glanced about the poorly lit room, counting again. Fifteen priests ringed them. Too many, even if they could free themselves. Biros unexpectedly lifted a fist, smashing the chorder. Clea stifled a gasp as the thin wood shattered, shaken by his senseless action.

"Your life is worth no more than this," Biros said viciously. "You will learn to attend me with respect." He regarded Clea for a long time before turning to Delos.

"You have something from Taland's workroom," he said. "It is mine. All of this is mine now. I have taken King Larok's place." He considered Delos. "I can take it from you, but it pleases me to have you present it to your King. It will change nothing, of course. My plans have already been made." His smile was cruel.

Delos, pale, bowed slightly. "But of course," he said. "You have only to ask. What is it you want?"

Clea saw that Senkhet's eyes glittered. He watches Biros as a cat watches a snake, she thought. But Biros is no snake. He is a bull, and a maddened bull can easily crush a cat. Or a kingdom. . . . She found herself swaying with fatigue and stiffened.

Biros rose lightly to his feet, pointing a deliberate finger at Delos. The broken instrument fell as he stood, and he kicked it aside. The pieces clattered across the tiles, the sound loud in the stillness.

"The amulet from the workroom. You have it," Biros hissed. "The one they use for their evil purposes. The amulet that calls the dead." He can't mean that, Clea thought with disgust, but the priests shifted uneasily, and a murmur of fear groaned through the shadowed room.

Delos showed frank astonishment. "If you mean the piece Marius stole, though it has no sorcery in it, I don't have it," Delos said. "The harbor guards took Clea's gold chain. Why don't you ask *them* about it?"

Senkhet stepped forward. "If I may address the King?" Biros swung toward him, his head thrust out. His jowls shook with anger, and Clea saw with a shiver that his eyelids flickered.

"You defile our sacred robes and yet dare approach me?" Biros roared. "Take this man to the temple and confine him." Two men leaped to obey, and Biros turned away.

"I cannot defile this robe," the Egyptian said

clearly. "You would be well advised to listen. Do not touch me," he warned, staring at the two priests. His eyes seemed to hold them, and their hands fell away. Biros watched Senkhet, his head tilted curiously.

"Who is this?" Biros murmured, as if to himself. "Who is this man, who comes from nowhere to defy me? This foolish man is no priest of Rhanjhon." He nodded. "I told you to take him," he repeated. "Obey your King."

"I am no priest of Atlantis," Senkhet corrected. "But Rhanjhon is worshiped elsewhere. . . . I am from Egypt, and in favor with its ruler." He's fighting to stay free, Clea thought, hardly daring to hope. "Surely as the ruler of this kingdom you must realize my value," the Egyptian went on, letting disdain creep into his voice. "Release me. I find these bonds tiring, and you wouldn't wish me to be annoyed."

Biros chewed his lip. "You came with these two," he said slowly. "Why should I believe you?"

Senkhet shrugged. "I came to consult with the king. It seems apparent there's a new king, doesn't it? You'd be wise to deal with me for your own benefit." He adjusted an earring with bound hands as he spoke, giving the impression of boredom. Biros's brow furrowed as he scowled, and Senkhet met his gaze squarely.

Clea lifted her head, listening. There was a clatter in the hallway, then voices. Could it be rescue? A small group of armed men entered the throne room. The men were dressed for fighting. These had to be Biros's rebels. So the city *has* fallen, Clea thought dully.

"Did you meet much resistance?" Biros asked calmly.

The commander of the men snorted as he approached the throne. "Resistance? The city is half empty, and the half that's left is on its knees, praying. The city's ours, but we meant to fight, not to net helpless fish." Contempt was plain in his voice.

Biros smiled. "But does it matter how a city falls?" he asked. "I am King now." He gathered his robe carefully and sat down again on the armless throne.

"Who are these three?" the commander asked, jerking his head toward Clea and the others. Clea returned his gaze with dignity. This rebel wouldn't see she was afraid.

"Why, they're part of my plan," Biros said, with a little wave of his hand. "My means of saving the island from our god's wrath. Their sacrifice will seal my bargain with him. Our people will be grateful." He leaned back to contemplate them, very much as Clea had seen him appraise a bull for a high temple ceremony. Her flesh grew cold. Biros was mad. Worse, he believed his own lies.

They were to take the place of the bull at the altar. The earthshaker would quiet down as it had always done, but this time would be different. This time, Biros would claim virtue from it. And the throne.

Biros droned on, and Clea closed her eyes. She remembered Atlantis spread out beyond the west balcony at dawn. The air itself was golden. She watched as the mist moved to touch the land, spiraling then to crown the sharp mountain peaks with equal grace. And she watched for the moment when the luminous light, strengthening, gilded the harbor. The ships moored below showed an impossible richness of color at that time of day. She wanted, always, to hold them in her palm one by one, reach out to bring them close to her eyes, put her cheek against sun-warmed timbers. . . . And now this most wonderful of Earth's kingdoms, this place of shining, was brought to a mortal wound.

A lamp sputtered noisily. Its uneven glow sparkled off the silver band Biros had stolen from the King. Clea's eyes grew hard. This priest, this usurping power-mad fool, had caused it all. He'd stolen the throne, but it was an empty victory, for the glory that was Atlantis would never happen again. She knew it. Time will destroy you, too, Biros, she thought, wishing bitterly that he could hear her.

Chapter 19

The three captives were taken from the throne room. Clea had asked to see her father, but the priest denied her request. "Oh, no, Clea." His harsh voice echoed in her mind. "You'll not join your father. Not just . . . yet."

She knew they were being taken to the temple, and for what purpose, but it all seemed unreal. The starless darkness, lit by bobbing torchlight, was peculiar. It wasn't the same warm cloak that covered the island each night, but something murky and disturbing. She was glad Delos and Senkhet were with her. There were only a few flames at the bottom of the hill. No light could be seen in the temples on the slope below.

A flicker caught Clea's attention. It was the reflection from the long sword held by the priest at her side. But how ridiculous, she thought dizzily. A priest wouldn't even know how to use a sword. A bubble of mirth began to swell. He could always use the sword to clean his face, she thought. Senkhet warned her wordlessly, and his rebuke amused her. What difference could it make now if she found an armed priest ridiculous?

See how foolish they look, with those great swords and the priestly robes? she argued. *Like cats with wings.*

It takes little skill to run a man through, the Egyptian sent dryly. *Particularly if he is bound.*

Clea's sudden wild gaiety dissipated. *We're going to die, anyway.*

Perhaps. It was Delos. *Senkhet, do you still have your knife?*

Ah. The Egyptian's answer held a certain satisfaction. *Biros forgot to have me searched. He's too full of his own grandeur.*

They were across the grass, at the smooth stone slab set in the ground beneath the arch of a temple opening. There were no steps here, for this was the way the bulls were brought for the sacrifice. The three of them would cross over this slab, just as the bulls did.

I can see you didn't convince Biros to release you, Clea accused Senkhet as they entered the arch.

Biros may hate us, Clea, but he mistrusts the Egyptian more, Delos sent.

The Egyptian smiled. *The night is not yet gone*, he told them. *And any dawn is beautiful.*

One small knife won't save us, Clea sent bleakly.

The temple was dark and ominously still. The sound of their passage was swallowed up in emptiness. No attempt had been made to light the wall lamps. The torchlight danced with the shadows as they stumbled down the hall. It was chill and damp, like an old tomb, Clea thought, full of crumbling bones.

The priest behind Clea pushed her forward. She

cried out, more in surprise than from the pain in her knees as she fell. She heard a heavy door being closed and the finality of the thudding bar. She twisted to a sitting position, tugging at her drape as she squinted into the gloom. Was this the classroom?

The glow of a fire came through a wide slit in the wall opposite the door. Clea realized where she was. It was the priests' robing room behind the altar. There was enough light to let her see a bundled shape in a far corner. Clea gasped when it moved. The figure jerked upright.

"Oh." The voice was familiar. Relieved, she peered at the figure.

"Nera, is that you? It's me, Clea," she said sharply.

"Clea?" Nera struggled to her feet.

"Who else would it be?" Clea demanded. She'd been frightened, and it made her angry with herself. "Are your hands free? Come untie me if they are."

Nera limped toward Clea. As she passed the glow of the altar fire, Clea could see that Nera was tied as well. When she reached Clea, she took Clea's bound hands in her own. Clea tightened her grip.

"It's all right. I'm all right, Nera," she told her. "Help me up. They haven't hurt you, have they?"

"No. But your father and the King. . . . I don't know where the priests have put them. They're going to kill us all, you know." Nera's voice was so calm she might have been talking about cutting grapes instead of the danger they faced.

Nera has accepted the danger, though she's done nothing to deserve it, Clea thought. She felt a thrill of pride at the courage of her friend.

"Bellini?" Maybe he could help them. It was only a faint hope, but Clea had to know.

Nera shook her head and leaned against the wall. She seemed older. "What could Bellini do against the others?" Nera asked. "I don't even know where he is. Do you think he's being held, too?" Her face was drawn and white.

"No, of course not." Clea's response was automatic. Her mind searched again for her father, but there was still no answer. "Of course not," Clea repeated more strongly. "Why would they lock Bellini up? He's one of them, as far as they know."

"I hope he's left the Citadel, then," Nera said in a low voice.

"Oh, Nera, he wouldn't do that. He wouldn't leave you here," Clea told her with a firmness she didn't feel. What did she know of Bellini, after all? Nera shook her head again and worked her way clumsily down the wall until she could sit with her head back against stone. She seemed resigned.

Clea bit her lip. How could Nera simply sit there, waiting for the end? She herself was possessed by a violent urgency. She wondered how long it would be before Biros sent for them, and as she did, the familiar tremor came. It's my father, Clea thought, with a surge of joy.

Clea, I have your father here with me. They put me in the room where he's been held. It was Delos. Why didn't Taland speak? Dread filled Clea's chest.

Is he . . . dead? she sent, swaying, and knew then that she had expected it. Suddenly hot, she watched as tiny brilliant points of light swam before her eyes.

No. No. Delos's voice was tense. *But he's hurt. He was struck above the temple, and he wants me to tell you that he can't communicate in the mindspeech.* The glowing specks faded slowly away, and Clea swallowed, nauseated. Not dead.

I understand, she sent, steadying herself with her shoulder against the wall. She turned away from Nera. *Will he recover?*

He doesn't know. He says. . . . There was a flurry and then Delos was back. *Your father doesn't know where the King is held, but he thinks he must be alive. He saw the King struck down. He says the blow came from Biros's hand. Listen. He wants me to tell you that Marius altered the sky charts. Biros ordered it done, to hamper your father's work.* Clea listened intently. Should this mean something? *He says some of the markings were changed, that he discovered it just before the attack.* Delos broke off briefly. *He says a star is falling. Bel. The star is called Bel,* Delos repeated.

An omen? No. Taland didn't believe in them. Why would he care about a falling star? One streaked down now and then, but what did that matter now? The blow must have confused Father, Clea told herself, disturbed.

Ask him what that has to do with us, Clea urged. *With Biros's revolt, I see no reason to watch a falling star.* Clea waited, and at last Delos reached her again.

Your father says Biros doesn't matter anymore. He says that Bel's course across the sky isn't like the others, and that it will strike Earth within hours. . . . When Delos continued, his voice was shaken.

Your father says we need to know, to prepare

ourselves. When the star hits, mountains will explode. Whole cities will be destroyed by flame, and the water will take the ashes. . . . He says the quarrels of men are nothing to this disaster, and of no consequence. Atlantis is doomed.

Clea was aghast. It was bad enough that Biros had taken them prisoner, but for the whole island to be destroyed for no reason? Oh, no, Clea thought, sickened. She didn't think she could bear it.

Ask if we could escape if we had a ship, Delos, Clea begged. She didn't doubt the star would strike Earth. Her father never speculated. No wonder the birds left, she thought, suddenly cold. Instinct had warned them.

Clea, if we had a ship we couldn't get to it, Delos sent. His voice was bitter. *Biros did that for us with his betrayal. Wait. I'll ask.* There was silence, and then he went on. *Those who take to the sea may live, your father says, though great waves and falling fire will take many.*

Delos, we've got to try, if there's any chance at all, Clea argued. There was no reply. Clea didn't wait. She knew they were trapped here.

She shut her eyes, her body rigid as she tried to comprehend the doom streaking toward them. The Egyptian had been right. Something vast and terrible moved across the sky. She held her bound hands out to stare at them, searching for an answer that wasn't there. Then she saw Nera watching her with weary eyes.

"Were you listening to your father?" Nera asked quietly. Clea nodded, too stunned to hide it from Nera any longer. With so little time left, it couldn't matter.

"So you've known about the mind-speech," Clea said. "Do you think we're evil, too?"

Nera sighed. "You're different," she said. "But your father is a good man, and so is the King. I could never believe Biros's lies." She was silent for a moment, looking at Clea curiously. "What did your father tell you that makes your face look like death?" she asked.

Clea took a deep breath. She couldn't tell her. The knowledge wasn't Nera's burden, but her own. Hers and the Skyborn's. If their end was to be even worse than Biros had planned, she could at least spare Nera this.

"He told me nothing. Nothing, but that we will die," Clea said severely. She moved to the far wall and sat against it, with her arms over her knees and her cheek resting on them. A bitter laugh escaped her as she remembered wondering how Taland could possibly think there could be anything worse than the capture of Atlantis. She tried to empty herself of fear so some measure of dignity would return, but exhaustion claimed her and she fell asleep.

Chapter 20

A nightmarish sound woke Clea. She sat up, her neck rigid. The fitful red glow in the room made Nera's cheek look flushed. She only stirred, but Clea's gaze flew to the door, which was opening. The sound had been that of a metal bar being drawn over stone.

Clea wondered if she had slept away her last hours on earth, sure that Biros had sent for them. A blue-robed figure slipped through the partly-opened door, pausing briefly before moving to Nera. A sword clattered against the floor as the dim shape bent over the girl, and a smothered exclamation followed.

"Bellini." Clea spoke, her voice hoarse. Her throat felt dry as ash. The priest threw up his hand to silence her. A knife flashed as he cut the cord that bound Nera's wrists. Then he lifted her to her feet, steadying her, before crossing to Clea.

"I couldn't come sooner," he murmured, freeing Clea's hands as he spoke. His pale hair was damp with perspiration. "I had to let them think I was one of them," Bellini went on. "They've been watching me. There's not much time. They've gathered at the altar. Biros plans to hold the ceremony at sunrise." He spoke in swift chopped sentences, his voice low. He removed his sword, wrapping it in cloth to keep it from clinking.

"My father and the King. Delos. Are they free?" Clea whispered, peering at him. He replaced the muffled sword in the sheath at his girdle, his face tight, and shook his head.

"You don't understand," Bellini said. "They've already been taken to the altar. The Egyptian, too. Biros sent another priest with me to bring you and Nera, and I struck down the man in the hall." He straightened. "If we go now, we can be off the hill before he's found." Nera was at the door. Clea was halfway across the room when she realized what Bellini had said. She stopped short.

"I can't leave them," Clea said helplessly. Bellini gestured impatiently.

"I tell you there's no choice. Do you want to die? You can't save them, and if we're not quick, Biros will kill us, too." Bellini reached for Clea's arm, but she drew back, avoiding Nera's eyes. Perhaps they could escape the island, but Bel still rushed headlong on its course toward earth. If there was any chance for Clea to escape, it would have to be with her own people. They would live or die together.

"Go on. Find a ship," Clea said. "Get as far away from here as possible in any direction the wind blows. Don't wait for the tide. I have to stay." She replaced the cord and pulled it loosely around her wrists. As she did she gave Nera a crooked grin.

"You're not telling me all you know, are you?"

Nera whispered eagerly. There was hope in her voice. Clea didn't answer, and Nera went on more slowly. "Will you be safe?"

"We're all doomed if we stay," Bellini broke in roughly, staring at Clea.

"I told you I want you to go, Nera. Go, now. Quickly," Clea insisted.

Nera bit her lip, her eyes enormous. She seemed about to speak, but suddenly drew a breath and was gone. The door swung shut behind the two of them.

I pray they find a ship in time, Clea thought grimly. They may have a chance.

She wondered briefly if she'd made the right choice. Even as it crossed her mind, she knew she could never have gone. She was Skyborn. As she sat down stiffly against the wall, feeling the hard stone floor, a short laugh escaped her. She, who had never been able to sleep if her couch were not smoothed, had slept on stone.

Tiny crystal bells began to chime. A slow murmurous chant rose beneath the bells' piercing sound. Clea closed her eyes, remembering the steps of the ritual. She'd only seen it once, standing behind a carved screen in the altar room. The vast room had been filled with fiery shadows. The chiming, slow at first, became increasingly rapid in a swirling clamor. Then the bells slowed again, dying, and the chant deepened, becoming a mighty shout that rang through the room. That was the signal for the bull to be led forth, and Clea had hidden her face against her father's shoulder.

She stared at the floor. It must be near sunrise. When would they come for her?

The door flung open, cracking against the wall, and Clea scrambled to her feet. Biros stood there. A second priest was behind him, holding a smoking torch high.

Biros looked carefully about the room. His gaze passed over the brass-clad trunks that were its only furnishing and came to rest on Clea. His voice was chilling in its parody of concern.

"So Nera's friend has taken her, and left you behind? Poor Clea. Ah, well, you mean nothing to Bellini. Still, Nera could have insisted that he save you. They'll be caught, of course. When they're returned to me, I'll be sure to punish her for leaving you to us."

Clea watched Biros warily, knowing him to be even more dangerous when he was pleasant. Surely he wouldn't content himself with taunting her. She pushed her wrists tightly together, pressing the ends of the cut cord between her palms. The other priest had a huge bruise from where Bellini had struck him. It was so hot her drape clung uncomfortably to her body. Too hot for Atlantis, with its freshening morning breeze from the wide green sea. . . .

"The door wasn't barred. If you'd been quick, Clea, you could have escaped." Biros sighed and smiled together. "Come." He stood aside. "You may join your father now. It is time."

Clea stiffened. Yes, time and beyond time, with so little of it left to them. A mantle of calm fell over her. "Thank you," she said clearly, walking past him through the doorway. His head lifted in anger, but it didn't frighten her anymore. There was no fear left, only this pure state of existence. Even as she wondered why she felt nothing, she was grateful for it.

The crystalline sound of the bells was more distinct now. Clea moved steadily toward the sound, indifferent to the priests that followed her. She watched her shadow's shifting progress as the smell of incense, peppery and sweet, infused the air. It seemed to intensify the dull ache in her head. The hallway ended too quickly, and she found herself at the altar room.

Clea lifted her head as she passed between the carved pillars at the entry, blinking in the dazzle of flame reflecting from the gold and brass that adorned the place of the god. The statue of Rhanjhon himself, ten times the height of a man, gleamed from the shadowed roof high above the marble altar. His molten beard curled away from his lips, as if he would speak.

Beyond the central figure of Rhanjhon, Clea saw the bed of flame that would receive the slaughtered sacrifice. The air was thick with incense, and through it all beat the bells. It was as she remembered, all of it, but this time there would be no stamping bull to be led in with golden ropes. Clea was giddy from the flames and scent, and swayed where she stood.

"Take her before the god." Biros spoke abruptly, carelessly. Clea looked at the altar. The captives were all there. The King, pale in his bloody drape, was supported by the Egyptian, while Delos and her father stood shoulder to shoulder.

Clea's mind cleared. Alert again, she saw that most of the priests were bunched near the altar.

She held her grandfather's gaze as she neared. His face was deeply lined. Senkhet appeared watchful, his lids drooping, and both Delos and Taland kept their attention on Biros, their bruised faces still.

Nera and Bellini got away, Clea told the others in a rush. *And my hands are free.*

I wish you had gone with them. It was the King, his voice weak, and Clea looked at him with concern. There was a certain hollowing of the temples — she had seen something like it before, and it frightened her. The great wound across the back of his head had matted his silvered hair with crimson. Biros did that, she thought, and a pulse began to throb in her throat.

I'm glad you're here, Senkhet told Clea, and Delos agreed with an almost imperceptible nod. *Your father can only communicate by speaking aloud, which is most unfortunate*, the Egyptian went on calmly, watching the room. *However, the King and I have freed our hands, like you. That will be helpful.*

The priest who led Clea to the altar joined with the others. The bells rang softly now, but the sound was insistent and somehow evil. Clea had a sudden violent urge to snatch the crystal pods and smash them on the floor, even if she would die for it.

How did you free yourselves? she asked, trying to take her mind from the bells. She noted that Senkhet and the King wore their cords caught about their wrists as she did.

Remember the knife Biros didn't search Senkhet for? Delos asked. *I wish I'd had one as well.* There was a wildness in his words, and Clea knew he was one of those who couldn't bear confinement. The

King's panther, too, had sickened in its cage.

Patient. Be patient, my young friend. The rebuke was typical of Senkhet, and Clea frowned. They didn't need patience to meet a doom that was already upon them.

Biros moved across the patterned tiles toward them, his robe swaying. Clea watched him come, bracing herself.

A flicker of movement caught her eye. She threw a quick glance upward. The puzzled face of the old one peered down at her from the hand of the god where he clung. She looked away, praying Biros hadn't seen. She knew Biros. He'd kill Boca before Delos's eyes, and smile. . . .

Chapter 21

It seemed to Clea that time had slowed to a snail's pace. Biros stood with his back to the Skyborn and his massive arms lifted. The flames in the golden bowl rose high. The priests were like bent shadows, their rods making sounds that cut the murky air. Clea wondered if they would ever stop.

Biros's harsh voice rose over the chant, and fell away only to soar again. It struck Clea's ears painfully. She closed her eyes to endure it better.

Clea. It was Senkhet. *I want you to cross in front of me to stand by Delos. You must do it quickly.* Clea hesitated, not understanding. *Now,* he sent sharply.

Clea obeyed, expecting the heavy hand of a priest on her shoulder. Something hard slapped into her palm as she passed the Egyptian. She clutched it tight, and turned her body to hide the knife she knew it must be. Scarcely breathing, she saw that their four guards hadn't noticed her movement.

What's this for? Clea cried out silently. *I can't kill Biros with this little knife. Even if I could, there are too many priests here for us to get away.*

I'll attempt to lower the odds, Senkhet sent dryly.

And for that, I need all our hands free. Clea listened, intent, as the Egyptian continued. *When the time is right, I'll interrupt the ceremony. You free Delos's hands then. Give him the knife when you're done, and he'll free your father.*

What good will it do? Clea asked.

Senkhet went on intently. *Clea, listen to me. The King is very weak. He'll need help to get out of here. I must depend on you for that. We'll follow you.*

But how? Clea's throat was tight with frustration. She turned her head to stare into his cool green eyes, which were glowing with tranquility and an unshakeable confidence.

I am Skyborn. If I say a thing will be, it will be, the Egyptian told her.

Clea knew he believed it. *If he's wrong, it will be a clean death, at least,* she thought bitterly. The King swayed, leaning heavily on Senkhet. His pallor frightened Clea, but he met her gaze and straightened. He even smiled, though Clea could guess at the effort it cost him.

You must listen to Senkhet, Clea, the King sent. *It's the only path we have except for submission.*

Grandfather, I will. As Clea gave her decision, doubt fell away. She felt free again and oddly cheerful. Was this the gaiety of men before battle of which she'd heard? *No matter,* she told herself, and watched the Egyptian closely for his signal, holding the knife firm in her grasp. *How terrible,* Clea thought, *that Father can't know our plan, that he's shut out from the mind-speech, like earthborn.*

The chanting quickened and grew louder. The sound of it rushed about the altar room like wind in a rage. Biros swung around to lift his face to the golden face of the god, his mouth contorted in the final roar of praise. The priests behind him flung themselves erect to echo it, in a deep resounding tumult of voices and bells.

The sound hung like heavy thunder in the room, but it didn't fall away into silence. The rumble continued, dim and threatening, and Clea thought the mighty statue quivered. It's this light, she told herself, flame blurs the edges of things. Senkhet stepped away a little.

"Biros." The Egyptian's voice was as hard and bright as a blade. The High Priest, his face flushed with exaltation, stared at Senkhet as if he didn't see him at first.

"You wish to speak, Egyptian?" Biros asked at last. "There is no need for speech. Rhanjhon knows you. You are acceptable to him." He reached out a hand, palm up. A shadow moved, and the long sacrificial knife appeared in his hand. Biros held it out, taking the tip in his other hand to study the sacred signs worked in the metal. "I would first honor our god with this gift from Egypt," he said thoughtfully. He gestured with a sudden nod of his head.

Two men moved together toward Senkhet. Delos shifted. His arm, brushing Clea's, was knotted with tension.

Smiling, the Egyptian swung his arms up and out in a wide sweeping motion. His eyes were brilliant, glowing. . . . They seemed to swallow the room and everything in it. Suddenly the cords that dangled from his wrists writhed, thickened, and grew dark with gleaming scales. Forked tongues darted from them. Clea gasped and the two priests fell back in fear.

Senkhet shouted with laughter. He pointed toward the fiery bowl at the altar. It flared high, then dimmed as the leaping flames became a great knot of hissing serpents. Someone screamed.

Now. The command was cold and clear. Clea slashed Delos's cords and stood, dazed, as he snatched the knife away and began to free her father's hands.

"Hurry. Get the King out of here." Delos said fiercely, his face intent. Biros shouted at the priests as they ran away from the terrible green gaze of the Egyptian.

Clea skirted the struggling mass of men widely to get to her grandfather. She pulled his arm across her shoulders. He was trembling with weakness, but he seemed amused.

"Senkhet has his uses," the King remarked, shaking with laughter.

"Please, Grandfather, don't talk," Clea begged, pulling him along. His gait was unsteady, and she prayed she could get him to the entrance. Biros could be heard over the tumult, threatening death to all who fled.

"Biros," Senkhet shouted. "What of your god now? Come and kill me yourself . . . if you can." Biros snarled and started for the Egyptian, his weapon high. He shoved brutally through the confusion of fleeing men. Clea pushed the King suddenly to one side as a tangle of robed figures fell in their path, fighting.

"Stop," Biros screamed, flailing about with his free fist. "There are no snakes. This is Egyptian trickery, you fools."

A deep grumbling roar began to rise above the

cries that filled the vast room. Clea gained the doorway, shaking, and stopped to look back. The King clutched a pillar for support. The tiles beneath their feet were vibrating and the massive statue shook violently now, rocking on its pedestal. Below it, Delos and Taland fought grimly against three priests who hadn't run.

Biros threw himself across the altar slab with surprising agility. Clea's hand flew to her mouth. Biros's broad face was a crude mask of hate. From where she stood, she could see his lips moving as he railed at the Egyptian. Senkhet stood, calm, a tall shining figure in the midst of the shadowed turmoil. Biros flung his long curved knife high, back over his head. Clea cried out, but her voice was lost in the clamor. Delos made a lunge toward Biros and then turned back to counter a thrust, shouting.

The blade paused at the top of its arc, splintering light from its edge. Biros readied for the murderous downswing. Clea's gaze was locked on the knife as it fell. All at once she saw a small dark object hurtling down, and Biros's blade flew from his hand. He stared at the vacant space where Senkhet had been. The Egyptian had vanished, like smoke.

"Ha!" Clea's grandfather spoke from behind her. The King was white, but raised an eyebrow in his old way. "Boca fights on the side of right," he cried, pointing. Of course, she thought. Boca had knocked the knife away! She whirled to look again.

Biros swayed wildly, shouting as he beat at the tiny creature. Boca bounced away and then jumped back to ride Biros's long hair. Delos was laughing. Now there were only two men against Taland and him. A crack broke across the tiled floor, and another opened to join it. Clea prayed.

Torches fell from the walls and flames scattered over the floor. Delos, panting, stood beside Clea. She stared at him.

"Come." Senkhet had appeared. And Taland. Clea's father suddenly pulled her away, but not soon enough. She'd already seen the statue of the god falling toward Biros, its curling smile mocking. Clea knew she would see that smile in her dreams forever. The floor shook violently. Delos and the Egyptian hurried, holding the King between them, and Clea's father ran close behind. *Rhanjhon has claimed his sacrifice.* The words drummed in Clea's head, but she didn't know if they had been spoken, or by whom. . . .

The King stumbled, fell. He said something, too low to hear.

"No." Senkhet's voice rang out. He knelt quickly, lifting Larok. "The courtyard," he ordered. "Quickly."

We must hurry . . . find a ship . . . we can't die here, Clea thought. She burst from the crumbling doorway. The sky was a brilliant green.

Chapter 22

"To the courtyard, Clea," Taland shouted.

"But the sky, Father . . . look at it." Taland pulled Clea with him. The ground moved under their feet. Clea could barely keep her balance.

"It's Bel. The star has fallen to the west," Taland shouted. An enormous crash — a ringing boom — deafened Clea, and she covered her ears in pain.

"The mountains." Delos's voice was thin. Clea stared at the tall peaks. One, the highest, was oddly misshapen, as though the top had been cut crazily off with a giant blade. A dark cloud lifted silently over them, spreading across the sky. Lightning darted eerily in the billowing mass.

"The island is dying, isn't it?" Clea's voice was flat, and her chest ached. Why had they bothered to escape? There was no time to find a ship. There never had been. Nauseated, she watched the ominous cloud move toward them.

"We must get to the courtyard," Senkhet panted. "There's so little time." The King's head lolled back, and his eyes closed.

"Do you think there's a chance it will work?" Taland asked sharply.

"I don't know," Senkhet replied, shrugging. "But if there *is* any hope, we'll need the stones. Ranson's stones."

Clea stared at Senkhet. Was it possible there could be safety in the ancient black stones that paved the inner court of the palace? That must be what Senkhet meant.

"Come, then," Clea said abruptly, running toward the palace without looking back. Delos was beside her. The once silken grass was now gray and spiky. It broke beneath their feet. The palace trembled; great cracks showed in its thick walls. Please, hold just a bit longer, Clea prayed, feverish. Just a little longer, until we can get there.

"Can we get into the courtyard through the gate?" Delos shouted. "If those walls come down. . . ."

Clea veered toward the high metal gate. "Hurry, Delos, help me," she cried, pushing fiercely against the latch. The gate was wedged into the ground, which held it shut. A metal fragment cut her hand.

"Over here. Push here." Delos shoved against the sagging center of the gate. Clea added her weight to his. They threw themselves against the gate repeatedly. It gave at last. There was a slim opening beneath a broken hinge. Clea sobbed, and Delos sat down suddenly, panting.

"See if the walls are still up," he gasped. She leaned through the opening — the surrounding walls were still standing.

"The blue space is with us," Taland cried.

"We shall soon know if that is true," the Egyptian muttered. He lifted the King over the rubble and into the courtyard, putting him down where the stones were undisturbed. Taland followed, and Clea and Delos slid through the gap after them.

Senkhet and Taland bent over the King. Clea looked at the sky, rubbing her eyes free of the dust that filled the air. The dark cloud the mountain had spewed was lifting. She heard sharp cracking sounds and narrowed her eyes, rubbing them again. Stones flew up from the maimed peak.

"Ah! Here." Senkhet held a dull red metallic disc in his hand. The flat, thin disc almost covered his palm. Clea stared at it. It was engraved with a formation of stars that were unfamiliar to her. This is what Marius stole, she thought. I remember it now. I kicked it across the workroom the day Father was in the golden mist.

Senkhet pulled a leather thong over his head. A similar disc was suspended from it. "I found this in a tomb," he said.

Delos drew a loud breath as Senkhet turned both pieces over. They were halves of a whole. The Egyptian looked up, his eyes burning.

"I believe this is the answer," he said. "I've looked a long time for it, Taland, once your charts suggested it might still exist." His thin brown fingers were busy, trying to fit the two discs together. They slipped into place, but the upper disc overlapped on one side.

"What is it? What are you doing?" Clea asked. Her father was intent, watching Senkhet shift the pieces, moving them a little. They still wouldn't meet perfectly. Perspiration beaded the Egyptian's forehead as he tried again. The hot ground quivered and rolled.

"Do you remember at the gathering how our people sent their force to witness your joining, Clea?"

Taland asked, and she nodded. How could she for-get? "The first Skyborn could send their bodies like that, not just images," he went on. "Why won't they fit? Could the pieces be warped?" He broke off, and then continued. "Senkhet was bringing the other piece to me. I knew he thought it might work when he told us to come here, to the courtyard." Clea's face was blank, and her father swung toward her. "Remember the force-lit walls Ranson's people used in their buildings? These black stones came from the same structures. If any energy remains in the stones, it should help the tool work. That is, if we're right."

"Twist it," Delos said hoarsely. "It needs to . . . Look, put the two together and twist. Can't you see?"

Senkhet manipulated the discs gently, rotating them. Clea heard the click as they locked, perfectly aligned.

"Touch me," the Egyptian cried. "Hold to each other. If this happens, it will happen immediately. . . . Let's hope it will take us all."

Clea snatched up her grandfather's cold hand and felt Delos grasp her other arm tightly. They formed a rough circle. The Egyptian began to fade into a golden haze, just as her father had done in his work-room. Her own arm was turning insubstantial and glowing. She could see the paving stones through it. The black stones seemed to be watching.

Suddenly there was a cry of disappointment from Taland. His outline was firming. They were still solidly there, all of them.

"No." Clea's grandfather spoke. He looked stead-ily at Senkhet and then at Taland. His dark eyes glowed in a face white as parchment. "Your powers are damaged, Taland. The tool can't take us all." He straightened and stepped back, joining Clea's hand to Senkhet's, and holding Taland's incredulous gaze. "I give you my force. Farewell, my son. Clea, my dear. Delos. And you, old friend," he added, looking at Senkhet with affection.

Taland's face was wrenched with anguish. "Father, no." He tried to pull free, but the Egyptian held him fast, while the golden haze built rapidly around them.

"It's too late," Senkhet hissed. "We're already going. . . . Let Larok do this."

"There is the work," Clea heard the King say, "and I will be with you, though you will not see me. By the blue space, I swear. . . ."

Clea stared at him, unable to realize that he chose to die with Atlantis. A furry streak, screaming, threw itself past the King into the pulsating glow that surrounded them — that they were becoming — and Delos grunted in surprise. The last sound Clea heard on her beloved island was Boca's scolding chirr.

They faded, wavering. The glow changed, brightened, surrounding them with pale silver gleam. The globe of the Skyborn lifted high above the fiery destruction that had been Atlantis, and the mountains fell in silence into the sea. . . .

Chapter 23

A burst of clicking drew Jama's attention to the brightly lit screen on her left. In all her time as an apprentice in the interstellar observation ring that topped Earth's APR Federation Building, she had never seen a configuration like this. She whistled.

"What is it?" The Observe seated across the wide white desk from Jama rose quickly, leaning across to see what she'd found.

"I don't know," Jama admitted. "But whatever it is, Zin, it's putting out an enormous surge." Her fingers were busy adjusting controls. They watched as the force bloomed, filling the screen with pulsating green.

"It's coming from an uncharted sector," Jama said, frowning. "An empty area. That's what puzzles me."

"Well, it's not empty now," Zin said emphatically. "Something caused a surge that size. They'll call the Obsmaster in on this one. What a find." He shook his head. "You have all the luck," he grumbled. "Me, all I ever do is track meteorites."

Jama didn't respond. Intent, she punched data into the banks to double-record the screen coordinates. "It's gone," she murmured. "I wonder what it was?"

"It's on record," Zin shrugged. "Let the Board figure it out."

Jama tapped the data to Obsmaster Mard, wondering what the Board would think about it.

The news of the find threw the Federation Board into a furor. They met immediately. The data Mard presented was — as expected — undeniably accurate, and the hologram taken from Jama's vidrecords was quite dramatic. The room seemed suspended in the air as the Board drew in a collective breath. Then it exploded with questions.

Chair Radik, usually dignified, called for order. He stood, attempting to be heard. "Please, quiet," he begged. "Order, please."

"Have you been keeping secrets, Chair Radik?" a member asked sharply. "Is there something going on out there that you haven't told us?"

"Why was the surge in that peculiar formation?" The question came from a historian.

"Please." Radik threw up his hands. "I know no more than you. The only thing that seems clear is that we must chart that sector. Then we'll have the answers. Is it agreed?"

"Agreed."

"Agreed."

The Board settled down. A ship must be assigned, a crew selected, and the ablest available commander briefed — all details were decided upon. Almost as an afterthought, the Board passed a resolution to commend Jama for her quick action in recording the force flare.

With the meeting adjourned, the members of the Board put their heads together to speculate on the meaning of their find — something the entire Federation would be doing until this matter was resolved.

Clea stood on a low bank overlooking the wide muddy river. She was thinking back to their arrival in this valley. After a tearful reunion, and a hurriedly called gathering, Taland had begun further experiments with the amulet. Clea's new brother worked with him. But Clea and Delos had done little but study for nearly two months, and she welcomed a free morning.

At least the history lessons are interesting. . . . It's my history, too, Clea thought. She stretched, feeling the welcome heat on her skin. Between classes and time spent with her mother and Leo, the ache of loss had begun to change into eagerness for what might lie ahead. She smiled, thinking how alike Delos and her brother were. Just like Father said, she thought. Boca chittered querulously at her feet, and she bent to scratch his back.

"Clea," Delos shouted.

Clea turned to see Delos running toward her from the direction of the temple. "What is it?" she called, puzzled.

Delos stopped beside her, out of breath. "Something's happening," he panted. "Your father's group is tracking something in the sky. Something big." He scooped Boca up to his shoulder, hushing him. "They say it's coming now," he added in a rush. "Leo sent me to tell you."

"Oh, Delos, no," Clea cried. "Is another star falling? Must we go through all this again?"

Delos watched the sky. "Your father says this object has a purpose. Don't you see? It *has* to be ours. Look, there it is."

An enormous shadow sped across the sandy soil. Boca screamed and jumped away as the cool shadow engulfed them.

Clea looked up. The vast silver starship passed overhead soundlessly. She thought she heard many voices, cheering.

"They've come," Delos shouted, jubilant. "By the blue space, we're found at last!"